**Here's what critics are saying about
Leslie Langtry's books:**

"Brilliant! Leslie Langtry has once again penned a 'gotta read every page' drama. I loved it, and the end as brilliant...Agatha Christie would be proud!"
—*Kings River Life Magazine*

"Darkly funny and wildly over the top, this mystery answers the burning question, 'Do assassin skills and Girl Scout merit badges mix...' one truly original and wacky novel!"
—*RT BOOK REVIEWS*

"Those who like dark humor will enjoy a look into the deadliest female assassin and PTA mom's life."
—*Parkersburg News*

"Mixing a deadly sense of humor and plenty of sexy sizzle, Leslie Langtry creates a brilliantly original, laughter-rich mix of contemporary romance and suspense in *'Scuse Me While I Kill This Guy.*"
—*Chicago Tribune*

"The beleaguered soccer mom assassin concept is a winner, and Langtry gets the fun started from page one with a myriad of clever details."
—*Publisher's Weekly*

BOOKS BY LESLIE LANGTRY

Merry Wrath Mysteries:
Merit Badge Murder
Mint Cookie Murder
Scout Camp Murder
(short story in the Killer Beach Reads collection)
Marshmallow S'More Murder
Movie Night Murder
Mud Run Murder
Fishing Badge Murder
(short story in the Pushing Up Daisies collection)
Motto for Murder
Map Skills Murder
Mean Girl Murder
Marriage Vow Murder
Mystery Night Murder
Meerkats and Murder
Make Believe Murder
Maltese Vulture Murder
Musket Ball Murder
Macho Man Murder
Mad Money Murder
Mind-Bending Murder
Mascots Are Murder

Greatest Hits Mysteries:
'Scuse Me While I Kill This Guy
Guns Will Keep Us Together
Stand By Your Hitman
I Shot You Babe
Paradise By The Rifle Sights
Snuff the Magic Dragon
My Heroes Have Always Been Hitmen
Greatest Hits mysteries Holiday Bundle

Aloha Lagoon Mysteries:
Ukulele Murder
Ukulele Deadly

Other Works:
Sex, Lies, & Family Vacations

MASCOTS ARE MURDER

A Merry Wrath Mystery

USA TODAY BESTSELLING AUTHOR
Leslie Langtry

MASCOTS ARE MURDER
Copyright © 2021 by Leslie Langtry
Cover design by Janet Holmes

Published by Gemma Halliday Publishing
All Rights Reserved. Except for use in any review, the reproduction or utilization of this work in whole or in part in any form by any electronic, mechanical, or other means, now known or hereafter invented, including xerography, photocopying and recording, or in any information storage and retrieval system is forbidden without the written permission of the publisher, Gemma Halliday.

This is a work of fiction. Names, characters, places, and incidents are either the product of the author's imagination or are used fictitiously, and any resemblance to actual persons, living or dead, business establishments, or events or locales is entirely coincidental.

MASCOTS ARE MURDER

CHAPTER ONE

"Excuse me," Betty said. "I'm going to have to wand you."

Barry Goetz shrugged and held up his arms as if this were a reasonable request from an eleven-year-old girl.

Kelly stepped forward to snatch the wand, but I stopped her.

"Hold on. He stole my lunch out of my locker once in 8th grade," I whispered. "I think she might be onto something."

"Welcome to the reunion," Lauren said with a smile to a woman who looked vaguely familiar. "I'll need to see two forms of ID from this list." She held up a laminated list that included passports and military ID.

"And we need a urine sample." Caterina blushed as she handed over a cup.

"Merry…" Kelly's voice had a warning to it.

Ava stepped up to Barry and waved a clipboard in front of him. "Do you live in town?" When he said yes, she continued. "You just have to sign this petition, and then you can go in."

Kelly growled, "Merry, what's happening?"

"Oh, that." I tugged on the hem of my little black dress.

I'd attended balls and galas all over the world in designer gowns worth more than the GDP of most third world countries, and yet I was tripped up by this one polyester dress.

"Ava's running for mayor and needs, like, fifty signatures. Can you believe there's nothing in the rules that says how old you have to be?"

"Merry!" Kelly's patience was wearing thin.

"Remember when we were kids and that donkey won the mayoral election as a write-in? I guess they later corrected that to say only humans could run. Still, Dorcas was a pretty solid mayor for the two years she was in office."

My best friend and co-leader threw her hands in the air. "That's not what I meant! I meant why is the *troop* signing people in to our high school reunion? *You and I* were supposed to do it."

I laughed. "Yeah right! I don't want to spend the whole party stuck *here*."

"That's what we were signed up to do." Kelly sighed. "You didn't want to be on the committees to handle food, drinks, or decorations. So we signed up for this. And it isn't for the whole night."

Betty's jaw dropped. "Not for the whole night? What happens if we leave early and Basque separatists show up and mow everyone down with machine guns? We have to *be* here!"

I wasn't sure how an unarmed Betty would protect a gym full of the people I had graduated with from terrorists with machine guns. "It's way better this way. Think of it like a service project."

Betty tackled Eddy Butz to the floor. "You didn't stop to check in!"

I was impressed. Eddy weighed three hundred pounds.

Ava scolded, "You're going to ruin that dress!"

"Not a priority." Betty readjusted her purple and gold velvet dress. "The security of Mrs. Wrath's and Mrs. Albers' reunion is *important*. They're really old and may never see these people again!"

"Where did the girls get matching dresses in our school colors?" Kelly had given up on chastising me, probably knowing from experience that it would do no good.

"I took them shopping yesterday. I still can't believe I actually found those colors."

"You knew enough to buy them dresses in advance but didn't think to tell me that you'd recruited our Girl Scout troop to do what we said we were going to do?" my friend accused.

"Of course I bought the dresses. Their parents weren't going to cough it up. I thought wearing purple and gold was a nice touch." I smiled as Lauren rejected Eli Bishop's driver's license as being suspicious. "And it's only these four girls. By the way, the girls are having a slumber party tonight."

"Good luck with that," Kelly snorted.

"It's at your house," I said before skittering out of her reach. That woman could move fast if you weren't prepared for it.

My name is Merry Wrath, and I'm an ex-CIA agent turned Girl Scout leader in my hometown of Who's There, Iowa. I'd originally planned on a full career with the agency, complete with retirement at 65 with the gold watch and everything.

Unfortunately, the Vice President of the US had a bit of an issue with my senator father so he "accidentally" outed me. That was very inconvenient at the time because I had been undercover in a dive bar in Chechnya, watching CNN at the very moment they announced that I was a spy.

At the time, my name was Fionnaghuala Merrygold Czrygy. So I changed my name to Merry and used my mom's maiden name of Wrath and, after a very generous settlement, quietly moved back home, hoping to start anew. When Kelly decided we should start a Girl Scout troop, I learned that there were things far more terrifying than being chased by Chechen nationalists and a chicken armed with an Uzi.

And most of them began with Betty.

"Go inside and have fun," Lauren said as she used zip ties on our sophomore class treasurer. "We've got this."

After Kelly set the former student council reps free and made the girls promise not to arrest anyone, we went into the gymnasium.

"This is the first time I've been here since we graduated eleven years ago," Kelly mused.

"About that." I tugged on the dress again. "Why are we having our tenth reunion eleven years later?"

"You didn't think to ask this until now?" Kelly asked with a smirk.

"Nope." Like I have time to worry about such things. I was busy recruiting four girls from my troop and buying them matching dresses.

She took my punch and set it on a nearby table. "The entire planning committee had mono last year. There's the bar. Let's go get a *real* drink. I think we're going to need it."

"Did you go to the fifth reunion?" I wondered.

"No, because you weren't going. What were you doing instead?" She gave me the date. How did she remember that? I couldn't tell you what I'd had for lunch, but the odds were that it was pizza rolls and Girl Scout cookies. That was my usual five out of seven lunches a week.

I thought about that for a moment. "I'm not sure about that specific date, but around that time frame I was undercover as a llama herder in Peru. Riley and I were surveilling the Shining Path terrorist organization. They had a compound hidden in the hills." I sighed. "I really miss some of those llamas."

"Just some?" Kelly's right eyebrow went up.

"Yeah. Esmerelda, Phoebe, and Jose were great. But that Fernando was a jerk."

Kelly did not ask me to explain, which was just as well. Fernando spit on me, stomped on my feet, and once, stole my oatmeal bars. His transgressions were unforgivable as far as I was concerned (especially because oatmeal bars kept me from having to eat the local food, which mainly consisted of roasted guinea pig). But the other three llamas were lovely.

Officer Kevin Dooley walked into the room, his arm up to the elbow in a bag of pork rinds.

"Oh, right." I rolled my eyes. "Kevin graduated with us."

Kevin Dooley was not my favorite person. He worked with my husband in the police department and, most days, could barely manage to compose a single thought. And he was always eating. Always.

The girls gave him a pass since he was law enforcement, and he looked at us dumbly before making his way to the dance floor, by himself, where he pulled off some moves that would be considered obscene in any Catholic country.

Kelly continued to the bar, and I followed her. "Drinks sound like a good idea."

Kevin, the paste-eating mouth-breather from our class, began waving the bag of pork rinds over his head. Then he started twerking. That's when my gag reflex kicked in.

Maybe it wouldn't have been so bad being stuck at registration after all.

"What do they have to eat here?" I asked as I took a glass of wine from the bartender.

Kelly looked around and spotted a long table. "Over there. I think we just have little snacks and cake."

"Cake?" I was walking as I said it. *Yeeeeeesssss!*

"Finn Czrygy and Kelly Albers!" A gorgeous, petite blonde cut me off by stepping in front of me.

Kelly smiled. "How are you, Cindy?"

Thank God for name tags. Sure, the name tags we used for the reunion only had first names for some reason, but it was usually enough to remind you who they were. Usually.

"Cindy Marsh?" I studied the woman. "You are really Cindy Marsh?"

The Cindy Marsh I'd known in high school weighed two-hundred pounds and was an extremely shy brunette with buck teeth and a spitting problem. This woman was thin with what could only be seriously augmented features in the breast and butt area. Her blue eyes and gleaming white teeth sparkled under the lights. Glossy, blonde hair cascaded over her shoulders and down her back in perfectly formed, beachy waves.

"I know," she laughed. "It's quite a change. How did you recognize me, Kelly?"

"I read your name tag," Kelly pointed out. "You know my married name?"

Cindy blushed. "Well, I live in Kansas City now, but I still subscribe to the newspaper here."

"You do?" I blurted out.

Why would anyone do that? *The Observer* was wafer thin and only came out twice a week. The highlights were usually reserved for the football games featuring the Fighting Whorish—an unfortunate amalgamation of Who's There and the main ethnicity of the first settlers. Sometimes, though, they promoted Girl Scout Cookies, which I considered to be far more newsworthy. The Whorish haven't won a game in years—especially against Bladdersly's Raging Bladders, our biggest rival.

"That's right. Oh! I should be calling you Merry Ferguson now, right?"

She really did know what she was talking about. I nodded. "Are you still Marsh, or…?"

Cindy made a face. "Yes. Unfortunately. I guess I haven't met the right man yet."

Looking around and judging from the number of guys staring at her, I wondered why that was. Maybe after the terrific upgrade, Cindy's standards upgraded too.

"Are you still a nurse, Kelly?" Cindy asked politely.

"No." Kelly grinned. "I work for a private investigator now."

Cindy was genuinely interested. "Really? That's very cool! And Merry, you had such a great career in the CIA! What are you doing now?"

The cake was calling, but when was I going to see Cindy again?

"I'm a Girl Scout leader. I don't really have a regular job." My own words stopped me cold. Did that sound bad?

"That's okay." Cindy winked. "You've already had a career more exciting than anyone else in this room!"

"What about you?" I asked. "What have you been up to in Kansas City?" She had to be a model.

She had the good grace to blush. "I did some modeling for a few years, but now I run my own talent agency." Cindy looked around. "Are you guys here alone?"

I nodded. "Yes, we are. My husband, Rex, is at a police convention in Reno. And Kelly's husband, Robert, is out of town."

"He's taking our daughter to visit some family in Minnesota," Kelly explained, as if my explanation was inadequate.

"I'm on my own too. But I have to say, I do have my eye on my old high school crush." She leaned in conspiratorially. "Kevin Dooley."

The world turned inside-out, and I was at a complete loss. Before I could say something stupid, Kelly rushed to reply. "Well, as far as I know, he's single."

Kevin was now sitting on the stage at the end of the gym with two plates of cake (that bastard got to the cake before me)—one in each hand. He looked from one to the other, as if he were trying to figure out what to eat first. Thing was, they were both gold cake with purple frosting.

"I think I'll go say hello," Cindy said. "I'll catch up with you later?"

Kelly cut me off before I could find a way to discourage the poor, delusional woman. "Absolutely."

As Cindy walked away, Kelly grabbed me by the arm and started dragging me toward the food—something she'd never had to do before.

"Can you believe that hottie is interested in that nottie?" I said as I began filling up a plate with cookies and cake.

"Well." Kelly shrugged as she filled up a plate with fruit and veggies. "I guess she's about to find out what he's like now."

I looked over to see Cindy sitting on the stage, chattering away as Kevin looked at her with hooded eyes and a blank expression on his face, as if he had never seen a woman before.

"Maybe we should've warned her," I said.

"She's a grown woman who can make up her own mind," Kelly insisted.

Betty signaled me from the doorway. I carried my sugar-laden plate over to her.

"What's up?"

If the girl wanted cake she didn't say so. In fact, she was all business.

"I have a couple of questions since we have a bit of downtime." She looked over at Ava, who was harassing a couple to sign her mayoral petition. The girl was promising to have free cookie vending machines set up all over town.

I'd vote for her.

I sat on a chair and began eating. "Shoot."

Betty cocked her head to one side. "What kind of situations justify using lethal force?"

I shook my head. "None. You come and get me, and I'll take care of it."

Betty nodded. "So you're our lethal weapon."

"Something like that, but I doubt you'll need me. I mean, seriously, anyone who willingly comes to a class reunion wants to be here, right?"

The child's right eyebrow went up. "What if you're in the bathroom?"

"Then you get Kelly. We do have a cop here. You can attempt to ask Officer Dooley."

Betty looked past me, into the gym. "Is he packing?"

I looked through the doorway to where he was still listening to Cindy talk. "I doubt it. Unless you consider cake a weapon."

"I think we should use signals." Lauren appeared at our side. "If something comes up."

"Like bird calls?" Betty asked.

"Too suspicious," Lauren answered. "I mean, there are no birds in here."

"Good point," Betty agreed. "We'll go with howler monkeys."

"Howler monkeys?" I stared at them. "That's your go-to?"

"Yeah." Betty shrugged. "Why did you shudder?"

I involuntarily shuddered again. "I did some time in South America. I don't really like them."

"Okay. You can leave now," Betty said. "I need to run a perimeter check. Do you have walkie-talkies for us?"

I hadn't thought of that. "I just thought you'd use your cell phones."

Lauren sighed and got her bag. She pulled out four walkies and handed one to Betty.

"Good thing you have them," I snorted. "Or I'd have thought Betty ordered them using my Amazon account again."

The girls looked at each other before looking at me.

"Maybe you shouldn't check your credit card statement for a while," Betty warned. "At least for a week. I've had my eye on a butterfly knife, and I'm too young to buy it."

CHAPTER TWO

Since I didn't know what to say to that, I went back into the gym and looked around for Kelly. Our ten-year reunion! Well, our eleven-year reunion. There had been one hundred and twenty-five people in our class, but Kelly had said only about fifty were attending.

Kelly was about twenty feet away, talking to a couple of women I didn't remember. Scanning the room, I didn't see many people I recognized. Those I did, I didn't necessarily want to talk to.

There was Barry, Eddy, and Eli, who'd all been hassled by my troop. The three of them must've come together because I didn't see any dates. I thought Kelly said Barry was married to a classmate, but I might've gotten that wrong by not listening when she was talking.

They'd been okay guys in high school—football players, I think. Kevin and Cindy. I choked down some bile that was rising in my throat. Lucinda Schwartz spotted me, touched her hair as her eyes grew wide, and quickly moved to the other side of the room. She was a television anchor on the local news out of Des Moines. A vicious girl, she'd tormented Kelly since elementary school—until the day she had the misfortune of being my lab partner in chemistry.

Lucinda wore too much hairspray, even back then. Perhaps the flame we'd been using got a little too close to her long hair. It went up like straw laced with lighter fluid. The teacher put it out with a fire extinguisher, and there'd been no burns to her scalp. She had to shave her head and wear hats for six months. But she never bothered Kelly again. I did feel bad for doing that and hoped no one here would tell Betty.

"Merry!" a voice squealed, and I froze.

"Hey, Veronica," I said, hoping I didn't sound too enthusiastic. I did not want to encourage her.

The woman burst into a fit of hysterical giggling. Veronica Bright, who had also been my real estate agent, believed that everything I said was the most hilarious thing ever. And while you might think that would be flattering…it wasn't. I really wanted to escape.

"You don't mind if I steal my old girlfriend for a moment, do you, Veronica?" a smoldering male voice said behind us.

"Not at all!" Veronica giggled, gave me a thumbs-up, and walked away.

I spun around to see Mitch Aiken grinning at me.

"Hey, babe." The ridiculously handsome man smiled at me "Remember me?"

Remember? How could I forget? Mitch had been the hottest guy in our entire school back in the day. Tall, dark, and handsome didn't even come close to describing the guy—who, by the way, hadn't even known I'd existed back then. And unlike most of us, Mitch Aiken hadn't aged a day or gained a single pound. It looked like he was wearing a bespoke suit as if channeling James Bond.

"Are you mistaking me for someone else?" I looked around. Or had he had too much to drink?

"Nope. Fionnaghuala Czrygy, I'd never mistake you for someone else." He winked.

He remembered my real name? Nobody did. They all called me Finn, except for Cindy, who'd actually looked me up.

"It's Merry," I corrected. "Merry Ferguson. I, um, changed it." My secret life as a spy was starting to get out in town, but it didn't seem necessary to talk about it to Mitch or anyone else.

He clutched his heart and, with a pained expression, said, "That's right. I heard you were married. I couldn't believe it when Marla told me."

My stomach lurched. Marla…my eyes grazed the crowd for that harpy. Was she here? The woman hadn't liked me, but then again, she hadn't liked anyone. Of course, Mitch might have liked her. They ran in the same circles ten…eleven years ago.

"Very funny." I forced a laugh. "How nice of you to tease me. Did Kelly put you up to this?"

Mitch seemed confused. "Put me up to what? You know how I felt about you all those years ago."

I wondered briefly if I'd wandered into an alternate universe. I wouldn't put it past Betty to have literally found and ordered one on Amazon, using my credit card. There was no way Mitch had had feelings for me in high school. If he had, I'd have dated him in a heartbeat. Now here he was, standing there looking all gorgeous and insisting we'd been an item.

For a moment, I considered lying and agreeing with him. It could be fun to pretend just for tonight. But then I remembered that I had a handsome detective husband, and I went with honesty.

"No." I shook my head. "Mitch, you never said one word to me in high school."

"I'm crushed that you don't remember, Merry. I really am." To my surprise, he genuinely looked it. "I always had a thing for you. In fact, I was hoping to see you tonight to rekindle things, but then I found out you're married."

This was starting to get a touch irritating. Was it because of his behavior now or my frustration that it wasn't true? Probably a bit of both.

I pointed across the room at the woman whose hair I'd once set fire to. "You dated Lucinda, not me. Remember? Seriously, Mitch, if this is a joke, it's in poor taste."

Kelly was giving me a strange look from across the room. Even she knew it was weird for me to be talking to Mitch Aiken. If I remembered right, she'd had a crush on him too. Oh, we didn't mind having crushes on the same boy. Dating him back then was never in the cards for either of us.

"I'm so sorry, Merry." His sad eyes locked on to mine. "I'm sorry you didn't understand how I'd felt about you. I obviously failed."

"Is this guy bothering you, Mrs. Wrath?" Betty appeared at my side.

"No, Betty, it's fine." I sighed. "Just someone I went to school with, like everyone else here."

"Hello, little lady!" Mitch bent at the waist and held out his hand. "I'm Merry's high school sweetheart, Mitch."

Betty narrowed her eyes and didn't take his hand. She looked up at me. "Want me to take this clown out back and teach him some manners?"

"Excuse me?" Mitch straightened up.

"Mrs. Wrath wouldn't have gone for someone like you," Betty explained. "You're what my mom would call *slick*." She turned to me. "I can kick him out if you want. No extra charge."

I stared at her. "No extra charge?"

The kid nodded. "You'd get a family and friends discount. I'm thinking of becoming a bouncer. Ava's gonna hire me to be her bodyguard when she's elected mayor."

Mitch looked from her to me. "She's joking, right?"

I shrugged. "I wouldn't mess with her."

"She's just a kid…" Mitch started to say as Betty grabbed his hand, twisted his wrist hard, and flipped him onto his back.

I stepped forward and loomed over him. "You were saying?"

Mitch scrambled to his feet and took two steps back. "Honestly, Merry! I just wanted to…I've got to go." He took off quickly, most likely hoping no one had seen him get bested by an eleven-year-old.

Kelly joined us. "What was that all about?"

"That creeper was bothering Mrs. Wrath." Betty smoothed down her dress. Then she walked away.

She stared at me in disbelief. "Mitch Aiken was *bothering* you?"

"Yeah! He told Veronica he was my old boyfriend." Heat rose in my cheeks. Was I blushing?

Kelly pointed at me. "You? He said he dated *you*?"

"You don't have to say it like *that*," I grumbled.

She shook her head, then closed and opened her eyes. "Mitch said he dated you?"

I folded my arms across my chest. "He said he had feelings for me—that I was the one that got away."

Kelly studied me. "Why are you acting so defensive?"

I threw my arms up in the air. "I don't know!"

Kelly gave the man the once-over. "He's got to be teasing you."

"That's what I said," I agreed.

"Maybe he has a concussion," she rationalized. "Or dementia."

"I don't think he's mentally ill." I frowned.

Kelly said, "It's just plain bizarre, which is why I'm chalking it up to mental illness."

"Merry!" Mitch called out as he scanned the crowd for Betty. "Later, okay?"

Kelly's eyes grew wide, and her mouth fell open.

"She's the only girl I ever loved," he said loudly to Eddy and Barry, who nodded solemnly.

I reached over and closed Kelly's jaw. Oh yeah, she'd had the hots for Mitch back in high school too. Every single girl had. At that time, Marla had pursued him, but he'd only had eyes for Lucinda. Something was up.

My best friend shook her head in disbelief. "What is happening?"

"Maybe he really did feel that way and just never showed it. Or he scored some peyote before he got here."

"I guess it's possible…" my best friend said. "I mean, back then you never mentioned even *talking* to the most popular boy in school."

I agreed. "If I'd had a fling with Mitch, you'd have known it."

Kelly looked around, her eyes settling on one person. "Well, Marla won't be happy."

I followed her gaze. Marla glared at me from across the room.

"The thing is," I said. "Mitch said Marla told him about my marriage."

"Huh." Kelly turned back to me. "Maybe she's over him. It's been ten years…"

"Eleven," I interrupted.

Kelly continued, "…which is a long time to get over your high school crush."

I decided to change the subject. "So what's the schedule for tonight? Is there a program, or are we just mingling?"

She shrugged. "Marla's going to give a little speech, then make some announcement. That's all I know about."

I was already done with all the drama. "Good. The sooner we can take the girls and leave, the better."

As we spoke, Marla walked up onto the stage. The event was in the gym, which, like most midwestern high school gyms, had a stage built in at one end. I never understood why they did that. Having a play in a gym was like going to a rave in an echo chamber.

She tapped the mic. "Hi, everyone! It's so great to see you all at our tenth…"

"Eleventh!" Barry shouted, and his friends chortled.

There was a split second of irritation on Marla's face. I meant it earlier when I'd said nobody liked her. Now *and* back in school, which was weird because not only had she been elected class president all four years, she had also been the homecoming and prom queens. Kelly once asked me how someone so universally loathed could win at everything.

"Fear," I'd told her then.

Marla scared the hell out of everyone she'd ever met. She wielded intimidation like a medieval morning star. Not only were her parents the wealthiest family in town, they also controlled the bank, the newspaper, and the local grain cooperative. The Zimmers wanted their daughter to excel at everything, so they "talked" to their employees and anyone else under their sway. It was the parents of my classmates who'd been "encouraged" to get their kids to vote for Marla.

Even now she had that arrogance. And while she'd been stylish in high school, now she looked like a prim, angry librarian with thoughts of global domination. Her hair was slicked back into a severe bun. She wore a designer black suit with spindly high heels and an Hermes scarf. She also wore a tiara, probably one of those she'd won eleven years ago. How tacky.

"Anyway," Marla glossed over the interruption. "Go Whorish!"

I'd hoped we'd get through the night without hearing that. Our team nickname was so embarrassing that in college I'd told people our team was the Fighting Irish—which, now that I think of it, sounds racist. It always amazed me that people accepted the name Whorish. But then again, there are a lot of things that people give a pass to—like tapioca, time-shares, and Russian figure skaters.

There was a very lackluster response as Veronica came over to Kelly and me.

"What does she do for a living?" I found myself asking Veronica.

Veronica collapsed in a fit of giggles that drew the unwanted attention of The Eye of Marla, whose icy gaze stopped her laughter immediately.

"She's a stockbroker in New York," Veronica whispered. "Her nickname on Wall Street is 'My Way or The Highway Marla.'"

That made sense.

"In a little bit we'll start the program that I personally wrote." Marla brought her hand to her chest.

Yay.

"Enjoy the food, but not too much." She forced a very fake, sad frown. "I have a special dessert prepared in honor of our lost classmate, Seamus Bailey, who was murdered."

The Eye of Marla settled on me.

She wasn't far off. No, I hadn't killed him, but a murder I was investigating led to his murder, so maybe she thought that it was okay to blame me for that. To be honest, *I* blamed me for that. Poor Seamus.

"But that's for later!" She laughed as if she hadn't just accused me of murder. "So don't eat everything—I'm talking to you, Eddy Butz!"

All eyes turned to the large man who Betty had earlier taken down in the hallway. He turned red under the scrutiny. However, this wasn't high school, so nobody laughed at Marla's cruel joke. That made me happy.

Marla didn't seem to approve of her joke crashing. "It's great to relive old memories, isn't it? Look at Cindy Marsh! That fat, slobbering girl is a gorgeous model now! Hopefully, with a personality transplant because, if you recall, she was dull as mud. Way to go, Cindy, on the transformation!"

Cindy rolled her eyes. Good. She wasn't going to let Marla make her feel bad.

"And then there's Officer Kevin Dooley..." Marla laughed.

Kevin looked up slowly like an elderly hound dog who's just caught a vague scent.

"I can't believe our class paste-eater is now a policeman!" She laughed.

Hey! That's my paste-eating policeman you're talking about!

Kevin shrugged and went back to eating cookies.

Marla now ignored the fact that nobody was laughing. Either she was overly confident of her cruel, comedic genius, or she had waited eleven years for a chance to attack all of us again.

"And let's not forget the worst football team in Iowa!" She pointed to Eddy, Barry, and Eli, who were huddled together. "The only thing worse than those guys was the terrible cheerleading that accompanied the games! Those girls couldn't even do a cartwheel right!"

Lucinda and her circle of friends scowled. Marla was making enemies faster than she had in all four years of high school.

"But I'm just teasing," she said quickly. "You know that."

No, we didn't.

"I know you all loved me. You chose me for class president all four years, homecoming queen, and prom queen!"

No one said anything. Her family was still a bit of a big deal in town, and there was no point in crossing them, even after all these years.

"Which is why, later tonight, I'm going to give awards to *you*." She smiled smugly. "For once, you are going to get the recognition that always seemed to go to me! And I've got some hilarious ones to give out, including some secrets from the past that most of you don't want revealed! But I will take bribes!" She laughed at her joke. Again oblivious to the fact that the crowd was getting close to finding pitchforks, tar, and feathers. If only they knew that Betty could score those things in ten minutes.

Her eyes scanned the crowd and settled on me. "And I've got an especially important award for Finn...I mean Merry Ferguson."

"She does?" Kelly looked at me. "Between this and Mitch, did you lead some double life in school that I didn't know about?"

"I've got something special for the girl who stole my boyfriend," she hissed into the mic.

"I didn't steal your boyfriend!" I shouted. "That was Lucinda!"

Lucinda went pale, and I added, "Sorry!"

Marla waved us off. "Anyway, enjoy the party, and I'll be back in a flash of Lucinda's burning hairdo!"

Lucinda turned and shot me a look. This time I mouthed *Sorry!* from across the room. She shouldn't be upset. She was beyond gorgeous now and a popular news anchor.

Maybe that was the reason for the burn. I recalled that Eddy had made a joke about Marla at an assembly once that had brought down the house. I think it had to do with Satan or the Wicked Witch or something like that.

As for Mitch Aiken, after ignoring her chasing after him, he had very publicly turned Marla down for a date over the loudspeaker at the homecoming game when he was crowned homecoming king. Was Marla getting even with people after all these years?

I mused, "Too bad a two-ton weight didn't fall on her during that speech. It would've been the most popular thing she's ever done."

To my complete shock, Veronica did not laugh. She grunted at me and walked away.

What did I say?

All four of my girls suddenly walked into the gym.

"Guys!" I ran over to the doors as they filed in, closing the door behind them. "You're still here?"

Kelly asked hopefully, "Aren't your parents supposed to pick you up?" She really didn't want them overnight.

"No." Lauren waved us off. "Remember, we're having a slumber party at your house." She turned to me. "Or at Mrs. Wrath's old house."

That got my attention. "I'm not planning on spending the night in my old house tonight."

"We hoped you'd say that," Betty said.

The thought of these four alone in my old house, where I'd stashed a lot of my spy toys and weapons, was too terrifying to think about.

"Why are *you* in *here*?" Kelly nodded toward the doors.

"The janitor sent us inside so that he could clean," Ava answered.

"What kind of janitor cleans on a weekend when there's an event?" Kelly shook her head.

Heaven help him if Marla found out. She'd have him fired, arrested, and possibly executed for messing with her night.

Betty piped up, "A ninja janitor."

An image popped into my mind of a ninja parkouring off the walls as he mopped so that his feet didn't mess up the floor. In a way, it made perfect sense.

"A ninja janitor?" Kelly put her hands on her hips. Her thoughts on the girls' imaginations were a little less open than mine. "You mean the night janitor. He's coming in at two a.m."

I looked at her. "How do you know that?"

Kelly rolled her eyes. "It was in the memo from the committee, stating we had to have the place cleaned up and be out of here by the time the night janitor comes on shift. Didn't you read it?"

"No," I said. "But he must be early if the girls met the night janitor now."

"It was a ninja janitor," Betty insisted. "He wasn't the night janitor. I know the difference. The night janitor is my mom's cousin, Carl."

"He was kind of weird." Caterina frowned.

"Weird how?" My spydy sense started tingling.

She shrugged. "He was dressed all in black. Even had a mask on."

I was running for the door before she had added a period to the end of that sentence. I reached out to shove the door open, but it didn't budge, resulting in me smacking into it. I backed up and pressed the bar again, but it wouldn't move.

Kelly sensed something was wrong and took off for the other exit, finding the same thing.

"The locker rooms!" I gasped.

Kelly ran to the boys', and I ran to the girls'. Locked. Both of them. We met in the middle in front of the bleachers.

"We're locked in!" Kelly whispered.

A scream went up behind the curtains on the stage, and we both ran for it. Kevin still sat there, alone this time, as a very pale and shaken Cindy appeared from backstage. She raised her hand and pointed from where she'd come. Kevin seemed to think he should stand, so he got to his feet, and she threw herself into his arms. He seemed confused, and then apparently it kicked in what you were supposed to do when someone hugged you, and his arms robotically closed around her.

I ran up onto the stage and behind the curtain with Kelly at my heels.

Marla was flat on her back, eyes closed. A counterweight—the kind used for theatrical sets—lay next to her head. Kelly went into emergency nurse mode and checked her vitals. After a few seconds, she looked at me and shook her head.

"Marla's dead?" I asked in a stage whisper.

Kelly studied the former prom queen's head. "Looks like one of the counterweights hit her pretty hard on top of the head." She reached around for the back of the spine, and the head wobbled loosely. "Broke her neck."

"Oh, no," I said. "Poor Seamus! Now we'll never have his memorial."

Kelly looked at me.

"What? I liked him a lot more than her." A chill ran up my spine. "During her speech, I told Veronica I wanted a weight to fall on her! But I didn't do it. You know that."

My co-leader rolled her eyes. She knew I hadn't killed Marla. "You were with me. I'm your alibi. Besides, this was probably an accident. Get Kevin."

"Fine." I pulled back the curtain.

Kevin was still holding Cindy, but also holding a bag of chips behind her, trying to eat.

"Officer Dooley," I said, a little proud of myself that I didn't say his title sarcastically. "Could you come here a moment?"

Kevin looked a little startled, but the haze in his eyes cleared, and he let go of Cindy to join us.

"Marla is dead," Kelly told him.

"Huh," Kevin grunted. "That sucks. They were going to bring out a special dessert to honor Seamus."

"I know, right?" I empathized until Kelly glared at me.

I pulled out my cell and sighed. I'd have to call the station. Thad Murray, one of Rex's new recruits, was back from the police academy and was supposed to be in charge. He could handle this.

"Um, Kelly?" I stared at my phone. "Do you have service? I have no cell service." I tapped at the screen. "I can't text, email, or use the internet."

She sighed and pulled hers out. Then she frowned. "Neither can I."

Kevin looked at his. "Same." He shook it and checked again, as if that was the way to make it work.

We were locked in the gym, Marla was dead, and now our phones weren't working.

And some people wonder why no one wants to go to their class reunion.

CHAPTER THREE

"Cordon off the body," I told Kevin.

"What do you mean?" Kevin seemed genuinely confused.

I heroically suppressed the urge to roll my eyes. "You're a cop. This is what you do. Figure it out."

He shrugged. "Okay."

Cindy was no longer sobbing as she sat there on the stage. Everyone else seemed oblivious to the problems we were now facing, which was a good thing, considering that the prom queen was dead with a broken neck just a few feet away.

I sidled up to Kelly, who asked, "Do we make an announcement?"

"About what?" I wondered. "The dead homecoming queen or the fact that a ninja janitor has locked us all in here?"

"Maybe one of them has a phone that works." Kelly clammed up as the girls joined us.

Betty narrowed her eyes. "Something's up."

I toyed with lying to her. I really did. But these girls were forty-year-old, battle-hardened Navy SEALs in ten-year-old bodies.

"We're locked in, and our phones don't work," I explained. "We don't have cell service. At all."

"Merry," Kelly said under her breath.

Did she think I'd tell them everything? "What? I didn't tell them about the you-know-what."

My troop had some experience with dead bodies since they popped up around me like weeds.

"I knew it!" Ava slammed her fist into her hand.

"You're holding out on us!" Lauren complained.

"Yeah!" Caterina added, rather uncharacteristically.

"Check your cell phones," Kelly urged in an attempt to distract them.

Four little girls looked at their phones, then at us, and shook their heads in perfect synchronization.

"You know," I said. "It's really creepy when you do that."

"Do what?" all four asked in unison.

"We definitely need to make an announcement," Kelly turned to me. "Someone here has to have cell service."

"I don't know." I scratched my chin. "Don't you think this will create a panic?"

Kelly whispered so that the girls wouldn't hear. "Yes, being locked in and the class president's untimely death may do that."

I shook my head. "I was talking about them panicking when they noticed their phones don't work."

Before she could roll her eyes, there was a loud clap, and the gym went quiet.

"Ladies and gentlemen!" Betty stood on the stage, holding the mic. "If we can have your attention, please."

"I guess that decides *that*," I mumbled.

Kelly stepped forward to speak, but Betty cut her off.

Her small voice was pretty commanding. Betty never did anything halfway, and adults never intimidated her. "The doors are all locked, your phones don't work, and you probably shouldn't drink the punch."

People looked at the cups in their hands. Did she say don't drink the punch?

"Uh, Betty?" I asked. "What's going on?"

Lauren nodded at her best friend, and Betty continued, "Yeah, you shouldn't drink any of the punch. Sorry about that."

I looked across the gym at the table where Kelly had set down my punch in favor of real cocktails. I'd guessed we'd dodged a bullet there. But what exactly was the bullet?

Barry started swatting at something in the air. Eli screamed and ran around his friends in a tight circle. And Eddy got down on all fours and started mooing.

"Betty!" Kelly took the girl by the shoulders. "What did you do?"

"It was an experiment," she said.

"For science class," Lauren added.

"We were going for extra credit," Ava explained.

Five former cheerleaders squealed "Touchdown" and launched into a cheer complete with splits that they obviously hadn't done in years. That was going to hurt later.

"It's creepy that they are all seeing the same thing." Betty pulled a tiny notepad and pen from her pocket and noted it.

"That's what we think about you!" I said.

Four heads turned to us. "What do you mean?" they all asked in unison...again.

Seven former football players gathered into formation against a team that wasn't there while the chess club began playing chess on an imaginary board with themselves as the pieces.

"I haven't seen anything like this since..." I started.

"You poisoned our class reunion?" Kelly shrieked at the girls.

Chuck Mullins, a guy who made fun of any boy who didn't play sports, began doing some pretty impressive ballet pirouettes. Sarah Bollinger, who actually had been a ballet dancer, began screaming and running laps around the gym, shouting, "Flying emus! The emus can *fly*! Run for your lives!"

"We didn't poison them," Betty declared as she continued writing in her notebook.

I snapped my fingers. "You spiked the punch with LSD!"

Caterina smiled. "You figured it out! I told the girls you weren't *that* stupid."

"The effects should wear off soon," Lauren said. "Hilly told us that—"

"Hilly?" The color drained from Kelly's face. "Hilly Vinton, a CIA assassin, gave you LSD?"

"She's not an assassin," I said automatically. Technically, the CIA disavowed assassination because it was wrong. Hilly totally did not get paid by the agency to kill people. But she really did. I'm just required to say otherwise.

I thought about the LSD for a moment. "What was the ratio she suggested?"

"Well, we'd estimated it for at least a hundred people. But half that are here, so…" Betty ducked to dodge a football as it flew past her head. "We might have used more than necessary."

Hilly had met the girls, and they loved her. And Hilly wasn't totally in her right mind. But she still shouldn't have given the girls hallucinogenic drugs to use on my classmates.

"This is your fault." Kelly pointed at me. "You introduced them to that whacko."

I nodded. "You're right. But I wouldn't call Hilly a wacko. She might be listening." I looked around, then down at Betty. "Is she?"

She shook her head. "No. She's in Peru for a beetle convention and doesn't get cell service down there. Kind of like us right now."

Cindy walked over. "What's happening? Why is everyone…" Her eyes grew wide as Venus Johnson began doing barrel races on an imaginary horse.

I looked at her. "You didn't have the punch?"

She shook her head. "I just had my teeth bleached."

That's when I noticed that there were about ten people who didn't have cups in their hands and were staring in horror at their classmates. They made their way to the stage and joined us. Mitch, Lucinda, and Veronica were among them.

Mitch ran to my side. "Merry! Are you alright?"

I stepped away. "Yes. I'm fine."

"I'm here for you if you need me, babe." Mitch pointed his thumb at his chest.

Kelly just shook her head at the wonder of it all.

"What in the hell is going on?" Lucinda shrieked.

"You tell her." I patted Kelly on the back. "I'm going to check on Kevin."

Cindy's hand went to her chest. "He had the punch!"

Great. What was I going to find on the other side of that curtain? Was our residential village idiot going to act like he'd lost even more IQ points, or would this go the other way and he'd start acting like a genius? I pulled the curtain aside and stepped backstage.

The body was, in fact, cordoned off...in a way. Kevin had put a ring of basketballs around her. He looked at me, holding a volleyball net. "I was going to drape this over her to hide the body." He placed it over Marla.

"You can still see her," I said.

The net hid nothing, of course. Kevin doubled the draping, but you could still see Marla very clearly.

I grabbed a tarp and held it up. "Why didn't you use this?"

He rolled his eyes. "Because it was in use holding the basketballs."

I didn't even waste any time thinking about that response. "Did you drink the punch?"

He pointed at an empty punch cup on the floor. "Yeah. Three cups. Tasted kind of funny."

Kevin Dooley was the only person here—and possibly anywhere, ever—who was immune to LSD. I'd be lying if I said I wasn't impressed.

Of course, I wasn't about to tell *him* that...

CHAPTER FOUR

After covering the body with the tarp and surrounding it with the little orange cones used with scooters for PE, I shoved Kevin through the curtain. The ten unaffected people stood staring at Kelly with open mouths as she explained what was going on.

The rest of the class was still doing their thing, whatever that was. I was happy to see that the football team appeared to be winning against their invisible foes. I knew this because a number of my classmates had formed a scoreboard with their bodies, and it said *Home* was in the lead by 200 points.

"They should pass out soon. Then they'll be out for hours," Ava said.

"Betty mixed melatonin in with the LSD," Lauren explained.

"At least there's forty people who won't be panicking." I relaxed a little. "That's a plus."

Kelly turned toward me, and the look on her face said I was an idiot.

"Of course, that's completely insensitive of me," I added for good measure.

Cindy had tumbled into Kevin's arms once more. "At least we have one of Who's There's finest here!"

Kevin looked around the room to see who she was talking about.

Lucinda began to wail, "Someone has locked us in here! Killed Marla! And is drugging us! We're all going to die!"

Ah. So Kelly had told them about Marla. I glanced at the girls to find them walking around the afflicted, taking notes. They must not have heard.

Veronica gave me a strange look.

"Technically," I said quickly, "we don't know that she was murdered. It could be an accident. And while we don't know who locked us in, and may or may not have murdered Marla, we do know who spiked the punch."

Veronica didn't laugh again, for the second time since middle school. That didn't seem good.

I regretted it as soon as I said it. Kelly's eyes grew wide. We couldn't tell them that four fifth graders did that. Word would get out, and then everyone would be going to them to score hallucinogens.

"Let's just calm down," I said. "This could all be a misunderstanding. The janitor may have locked the doors, forgetting we were in here. And the counterweight could've just fallen on Marla and broken her neck."

Veronica's right eyebrow went up. So she hadn't forgotten that I'd said maybe a weight should fall on Marla and crush her.

The group considered what I'd said. I guess it wasn't too surprising that no one seemed to mourn Marla.

"But what if it's not that?" an extremely tan, leathery blonde woman I didn't recognize asked.

I stared at her name tag. "Judy? Judy Jones? Is that you?" This aged-beyond-her-time woman had been a sweet kid who played with me and Kelly in elementary school. We'd drifted apart in middle school, and I had no idea what she'd done with herself after graduation. Apparently, she spent a lot of time in the sun.

Judy smiled, and her face crinkled into a well-worn leather. "Hi, Merry. I'd meant to say hi before." She motioned at the crowd on the floor, who were now singing and dancing to "YMCA." That's new. LSD usually affects people differently. But these guys were in sync. I'd have to ask Hilly about that. Just think of the possibilities!

I turned to Dooley. "What do you think, Kevin?"

He scratched his head. "I don't know. But I think we should ask that law enforcement professional Cindy mentioned."

"She's talking about you," I hissed.

Kevin's face lit up with recognition of the fact that he was, in fact, a police officer. "Do you want me to arrest someone?" He pointed at the folks on the floor, who were now involved in a huge game of Twister. He pulled out a pair of handcuffs.

Who brings handcuffs to a high school reunion?

"You can't arrest them," Lucinda gasped. "They're the victims here. And Marla, of course."

Kevin pulled me aside. "Can you tell me who to arrest, then? I don't usually make these decisions."

It was the most coherent thing I'd ever heard him say.

"Arrest them for what?"

"That murder thing." He pointed to the curtain.

"We don't know it's murder." An idea popped into my head. "Let me check something. Be right back."

After announcing that if anyone had any questions, they should direct them to Kelly, I headed backstage. A ladder bolted to the wall led to a catwalk overhead, where the ropes were tied for the counterweights. I started climbing.

It seemed to me that if I found some evidence of tampering, I could call this a murder. If not, it was an accident. Then the next step would be to do something about my deranged classmates on the gym floor, find a way out of the gym, and get help.

The bolts that held the ladder against the wall seemed a bit too wobbly for my taste, but if the school thought it was safe for students, it would be safe enough for me, right? Just as I hit the last step at the top, there was a squeak, and the ladder loosened considerably. In fact, I barely managed to dive for the catwalk before the whole thing crashed to the ground.

I added "getting down from a very high place" to my list of things to do.

"Merry?" Cindy and the girls appeared at the bottom.

Dammit. I didn't want them to know about the body.

"Hey." Betty pulled aside the tarp and yelled up, "There's some dead chick down here."

"Good thing the ladder missed her," Caterina said. "That would've been gross."

"I'm alright," I shouted down, answering the question no one had asked.

"Kelly told me to tell you to stop doing whatever it was you did to make that noise," Cindy shouted back. Her eyes went to the ladder. "I guess it wasn't your fault."

The girls were studying the deceased. They wouldn't touch anything. They knew the drill. But then again, they were overly curious. Too curious. I needed to find a way down.

"Keep an eye on the girls," I shouted.

Giving Cindy something to do would help distract her. Hopefully. She nodded and started talking to the girls.

Well, since I was up here, I might as well see what had happened. I shook the catwalk gently, but it seemed to be sound enough. Slowly, I made my way to the ropes and got down on my knees to examine them.

Four ropes were tied snugly around a metal bar. The weights beneath them were held firmly in place. One rope was dangling. I leaned forward and made a grab for it. My fingers grasped the rope, and I pulled it toward me.

"Damn," I muttered.

Betty shouted, "I knew it!"

"How did you get that from one word," I shouted down.

"Because with you it's always murder."

That kid was way too smart. This was not in our best interest. Marla was murdered all right. Because this rope wasn't frayed.

It had been deliberately cut.

CHAPTER FIVE

"How are you going to get down from there?" Cindy yelled.

"No problem," I shouted back. "Piece of cake!"

I had no clue how I was going to get down. I just didn't want to worry anyone. The only ladder had come off the wall. And I was too high up to jump. Well, I could jump, but then I'd break an ankle…or two or even more than that.

Once, in Budapest, this MI6 agent and I were running from some rather unsavory characters from the Turkish embassy when we were trapped on top of a two-story high roof. Bob, the MI6 guy, decided to jump for it and landed on top of an old sewing machine someone had dumped in that alley (it was literally the only thing in the alley). Broke both legs, his right index finger, and his coccyx. He hadn't even landed on his coccyx.

But that's not why his colleagues tease him. They give him a hard time because there was a fire escape ladder (which I took) right next to where he had jumped. I do feel a little bad for filming his fall on my cell and sharing it with MI6. They actually use it as a safety video now.

There were a handful of ropes tied to the scaffold that reached almost to the floor. Could I shimmy down one of those? I wasn't sure. I never mastered rope climbing. But this was more like falling while holding on to a rope…right?

Kelly joined the girls and looked at me. "How are you going to get down?"

"Cindy already asked that," I shouted back a bit more irritably than I'd intended

"You suck at ropes," she shouted back. Kelly knew. She'd seen me fail at this in gym class for eleven years.

"I know," I grumbled.

"Too bad there isn't a tree you could fall out of." Kelly smirked, referring to a time I fell out of a tree and hit every branch on the way down.

I pretended she hadn't said a thing. "Could you just look around for a ladder or something helpful, please?"

Kelly said something to the girls, and they split up into two groups—stage right and stage left.

"What did you find out?" Kelly shouted.

"It was murder," Betty answered for me.

"The rope was cut," I yelled down.

Kelly seemed surprised. "You touched it with your hands?"

I looked at the rope. "I don't think you can fingerprint rope," I replied a bit dubiously.

I'd been so careful about not touching the body. Why hadn't I done the same for the rope? Oh well. I could explain it to the forensics team later. Unless I'm the suspect. Then this looks pretty damning.

The girls returned empty-handed, but offered some ideas on how I could return to the floor.

"You could try to fly," Caterina suggested.

Kelly shook her head. "People can't fly."

Caterina smiled encouragingly. "How do you know? Maybe she'll be the first one who does."

Ava shouted, "What if we make a zip line?"

Lauren frowned. "How can we build that if we can't get up there?"

"I can teach you some pointers on poofing," Betty offered. She'd been working on magic for a little while now and had learned how to appear and disappear at will—a scary notion for anyone, but extremely terrifying when eleven-year-old Betty did it.

"Have you ever poofed from this height?" I asked.

"No. I'm pretty sure that would be certain death," Betty replied.

I sighed. "Then why did you suggest that to me?"

She shrugged. "I thought it would be an interesting experiment."

Lauren threw her arms in the air. "Two extra credit science projects! Woo-hoo!"

The girls began high-fiving each other.

"None of these are really helpful," I called down. "I'm going to risk the ropes."

A gasp went up from below. I chose a rope, and everyone stepped back.

"You're not going to spot me?" I called down to my best friend.

Kelly took a step back. "No, I'm avoiding you landing on and killing me."

"I'll catch you!" Caterina, our sweet girl, stepped forward, but Kelly dragged her away.

"Wait!" Cindy held a finger up and then ran off. She returned a minute later with Kevin, dragging a gymnastics mat. They placed it under the rope. "Try to aim for that."

It had to be four inches thick—which did not seem thick enough.

"You have to hurry!" Cindy shouted. "Our drugged classmates are having an imaginary food fight!"

I hoped that meant they were using imaginary food. I was getting hungry. Our conscious classmates started swarming backstage. Lucinda was trying to get frosting out of her hair.

"It's insane out there!" she shouted. "We figured it would be safer back here." She looked at the body and then the ladder on the floor.

I took the rope into my hands, whispered a silent prayer, and jumped forward, grabbing it with my legs. I hung there, trying to figure out how to drop without getting rope burn. I probably should've thought about that before.

The rope shook. That was odd. I looked up to see another darkened catwalk even higher above me. A shadowy, gloved hand held my rope while another hand flashed a knife and began slicing.

"Someone's up there!" I screamed.

"Where?" came Kelly's call.

"Above me! They're cutting the rope!"

"Why? We already know the other rope was cut," Kelly began to reason. "What's the point of killing you?"

"While I appreciate your trying to reason this out," I snapped, "I'd love it if you'd catch me when I fall."

"Nope" came the reply. "I've got a toddler who needs me. Just slide down."

The rope was seriously wriggling as the person above sawed faster upon hearing our exchange. Hand over hand, I started to lower myself to the floor. I really didn't want to slide down and risk rope burn.

There was six feet left when the rope broke, and I fell the rest of the way, landing on the side—where the mat wasn't. The wind was knocked out of me, and I lay there trying to catch my breath.

"What did you do that for?" Ava stood over me. "You were supposed to land on the mat!"

I wondered that myself as I heard our doped-up classmates singing the Whorish fight song en masse on the other side of the curtain. But perhaps the more important question was, why had someone murdered Marla, locked us in, and then tried to kill me? Okay, so that's three questions.

Cindy dragged Kevin over, and he looked down at me. Mitch followed.

"Merry!" he cried out as he knelt beside me, taking my hand in his. "Are you okay?"

"Someone's up there!" Cindy pointed at the ceiling. "And he tried to kill Merry!"

Kevin slowly looked up, causing his mouth to stay open as only the upper part of his head went back. He kind of looked like a Muppet.

Then he looked at me. "Who was it?"

I sat up. "I have no idea. I don't even know how they could've gotten up there."

Kevin shrugged. "Probably through the roof. There's a trap door on the roof that leads there."

I stared at him. "That seems like important information we should've had when we told you we were locked in."

"Huh." Kevin scratched his head. "I didn't think about that. Do you know where that dessert was stashed? The one we were going to eat for Seamus?"

It didn't surprise me that Kevin reacted this way when up above us on the roof was a killer. What did surprise me was that his idiocy did nothing to dim the admiration in Cindy's eyes. As soon as I made sure that I hadn't broken any bones, I needed to have a talk with her.

Mitch lifted me to my feet. "So the trap door on the roof goes to the second catwalk? I could climb up and get him."

I rubbed the back of my head. "The only rope connecting the two catwalks is the one I fell off of, and there aren't any ladders. I guess that's why they had the door on the roof." Mitch reached out to touch my face, and I slapped his hand away. "You know, I just don't get why we have no cell service here. How did they knock that out?"

Mitch laughed. "These old high school gyms are like nuclear bunkers. I've never heard of one built after World War II that wasn't like this."

I stared at him. "What do you mean?"

He shrugged. "Don't you remember all the signs that said the gym was a civic shelter?"

"I do remember those signs." I wondered why I hadn't thought of that before.

Mitch continued, "For these schools built during the Cold War, the gyms were designed to be sturdy enough to withstand bomb blasts. At least, that's what they thought back then."

It dawned on me. "So the killer isn't responsible for the lack of cell service. This is just a building issue."

"That's right," Mitch agreed. "We just don't remember it because we didn't have cell phones in high school."

In a weird way, it was a relief that our phones didn't work because of the way the school was built. It wasn't helpful, but at least we knew our killer didn't have some sort of mystery machine.

The girls were wheeling a chalkboard over to us. Lauren handed me some chalk.

"For our murder board," she explained. "If we're going to be locked in here until two in the morning, we might as well do a murder board."

My troop loved making murder boards so much that sometimes they made them when there weren't any unnatural deaths. For the imaginary murders, the killer always seemed to be me. Kelly was never the killer. Not even once.

"You guys start it. I'm going to see what's going on out there." That should keep them busy.

It had become very quiet in the gym. I didn't like it.

As I stepped out onto the stage, I realized why. All of the previously crazed people were passed out on the floor. The others filed out behind me, their eyes bulging when they realized their classmates were out cold.

"Did you say someone tried to kill you?" Judy's eyes grew wide.

"Did you say Marla really was *murdered*?" Lucinda's hand went to her heart.

Kevin squinted at the bodies on the gym floor. "Are those guys dead?"

Kelly gasped as she ran past me to the gym floor and checked the pulse of one of our female classmates. She sighed, indicating that she wasn't dead. Then she went from person to person, checking everyone. When she got to the last guy, she frowned.

Barry Goetz looked like everyone else passed out on the floor. She checked the pulse in his neck. Then she stood up and looked at me. She shook her head.

I was next to her in a flash, running my hands over the body, which I knew I wasn't supposed to do, but didn't really care anymore. Kneeling in a little black dress was a bad idea. Why hadn't I just worn sweats? Kelly had told me I couldn't, but I shouldn't have listened to her.

"Heart attack?" I asked hopefully as I tugged on my hem.

"I wish." She reached past me and pulled down the collar of his dress shirt. "Ligature marks."

"Barry was strangled?" I deflated. "The killer strangled him? While we were backstage?"

She nodded. "He's still warm."

"How did the killer get from the roof to in here so quickly?"

"Well, we were all standing around you for a bit..." Kelly reasoned.

"That could mean..." I ran for a door, asking the girls to check the other doors. Maybe the killer had forgotten to lock them.

No such luck. We were still locked in. With thirty-nine passed out people, two stiffs, and four little girls. It was possible that the killer could've raced back down here, unlocked the door, and strangled Barry. But was it probable? Did the killer have help?

The folks on the stage didn't take the news well. Killing that bitchy Marla was one thing, but Barry's death suggested that the killer wasn't done with us. To calm everyone down, I asked each of them to give statements to the girls. To my surprise, they were all eager to be interviewed. The girls took it seriously, asking the right questions, except for *Why didn't you drink the punch?*

Kelly threw a tablecloth over Barry, but didn't move him. The others, who were all alive, we arranged into more comfortable positions.

"How long will they be unconscious?" she asked me.

"I think a few hours at least." I was trying to use one of Cindy's hairpins to see if I could pick the boys' locker room door.

"But they're just lying there, vulnerable to being picked off." Kelly was concerned. As a former nurse she still had that *do no harm* commitment.

"I don't think the killer will do anything else with all of us in here." But just to be safe, I called Mitch over and asked him to stand guard over our unconscious classmates.

"I'll keep them safe, Merry," he vowed before crushing me into a hug. "You be careful! I don't want to lose you!" And then he walked over to a table, turned a chair around to sit in, and began surveillance.

Kelly watched him go and picked up on where we had left our conversation. "But he did. The murderer killed Marla and Barry with all of us in here."

"Yes," I sighed. "But our attention was elsewhere. Not like now."

Those still conscious sat on the edge of the stage in a state of shock. The girls were writing furiously on the chalkboard, and Kevin was drinking more punch, which still unfairly had no effect on him. Cindy stood by his side looking nervous.

The hairpin broke, and I swore out loud. Kelly didn't even chastise me, which was really strange. She was really struggling with this. I sat down on the floor, and she joined me.

"I don't think I'll go to any more reunions," I said.

"I don't blame you," Kelly agreed. "If we ever get out of here alive."

"Of course we'll get out of here alive. There's only one killer," I said for her benefit. No point in telling her my theory that there might be more. "And there's still fifty-two of us."

She looked confused. "There were fifty of us, minus Marla and Barry." She thought for a moment. "And the bartender."

I held up my index finger. "Plus four girls. That makes fifty-three. And I like those odds. We can take on the killer. Hell, Betty could take on the killer and win."

Kelly brightened a bit. "That's true. Well, not the Betty part. I'm not going to let her fight off a murderer."

"Then let's concentrate on what we know," I suggested. "We know that Marla gave a speech that not only insulted almost everyone here, but she threatened to expose secrets later. We know we are locked in here and that our phones don't work. We know that Marla was murdered and that the killer tried to kill me and succeeded in killing Barry."

Kelly chewed her lip. "Do you think someone is planning to kill us off one by one?"

I understood her concern. That actually happened to us before, on an island during a storm. But we came out of that alright in the end.

"If they wanted to kill us one at a time, there are far more effective ways to pull that off. They could gas us. Set fire to the school. They could…"

Kelly held up her hands. "Stop. Don't give the killer any ideas."

I wondered. "Maybe Barry figured out who the killer was and confronted him."

"As out of his mind as he was?" Kelly looked skeptical.

"Or the killer *thought* Barry figured it out. Or spotted him. It could be he'd planned to make it look like Marla's death was accidental, but Barry somehow called him out."

Kelly frowned. "Which would mean now he's desperate."

I nodded. "What we need to do is stick together, try to get out of here, and get help."

We sat in silence as we pondered this. Our biggest issue would be if someone started to panic. We had to keep everyone calm. Maybe the girls could teach everyone some scout songs.

"When we do get out of here, someone needs to stay to protect those on the floor," Kelly said.

"There you go!" I patted her on the back. "That's positive thinking!"

She sighed and leaned back against the wall. "What time do you think it is?"

"Don't you wear a watch?"

Kelly shook her head. "Neither do you. No one does anymore."

I thought about this for a moment. "I'd estimate it's probably 7:30."

My best friend looked impressed. "Is that some spy skill?"

I shook my head. "No. I'm totally guessing. With no windows in here, it's pretty hard to tell."

Kelly chewed her lip. "What do we do for light if the power goes out?"

I hadn't thought of that. "The flashlight app on the phones should still work, right? But why don't you check with the others and see if anyone has some sort of flashlight on them, just in case."

It was busy work, and I think she knew it, but I wanted to walk the perimeter of the gym. As I went, I tested the doors but still found them locked. There was a door that said *Janitor*, but it too was locked. I climbed up into the bleachers, between the two locker rooms, to the highest point and sat there, looking down at the layout.

The two main entrances framed the lobby and the registration area. This was where the girls had been told to go into the gym by the ninja janitor. To the left was the stage and the display table that held old yearbooks in a weak attempt at a display. To the right, in the corner, was the food and punch. Between that and the bar on my side were seven round tables. On my left was the sound system for the music.

On the floor in front of the stage were the unconscious bodies of my classmates and one dead one. Marla's body was still backstage.

Kevin lumbered toward me. I watched as he slowly ascended the bleachers and sat down beside me.

"What's next?" he asked.

I stared at him. "Why are you asking me? *You're* law enforcement."

He nodded. "Yeah, but I've decided that you're the boss. What's next?"

I wasn't entirely surprised that he was putting this on me, and in a way, I kind of respected his honesty in realizing he was in way over his head. But Kevin and I had always had a sort of adversarial relationship. And now he wanted to partner up? Was it because my husband was his boss, or was he really unable to take charge?

"You've solved a lot of murders," he continued. "More than me."

I studied him. "You've solved murders?"

He shook his head. "No."

"Well, Kevin." I sighed. "Here's what we've got so far. Someone murdered Marla by cutting the rope on a counterweight backstage. It fell on her and broke her neck."

"Why would anyone kill Marla?" he asked.

Seriously? "She insulted pretty much everyone in her speech and promised to reveal secrets later. That seems like a good motive."

He took a sip from his punch but said nothing.

"Then the killer cut the rope as I was climbing down..."

He looked at me curiously. "Why did they do that? *You* didn't say anything at the announcements."

"Huh," I said. "That might dispel the idea that someone killed Marla for revenge or to shut her up."

Kevin's eyes slowly widened, like a bloodhound who's just woken up from a coma. "He tried to stop you from finding out it was murder!"

"Okay," I said slowly. "That might work if I was killed on the way up. I'd not only found the cut rope, but I'd also already announced it to everyone below."

When he didn't speak, I continued.

"And then there's Barry's murder..."

Dooley's mouth dropped open. "Barry was murdered?"

"You know what, Kevin?" I patted his arm. "You're right. I'm good at detecting. You just stand by until I need you to arrest someone."

Kevin's eyes found Barry's body, covered on the floor. "He owed me $20."

"I'm sorry for your loss," I said with complete sarcasm that went over his head.

Kevin got to his feet. "Maybe I can get it from his mom or something at the funeral."

I had to ask, "Why did you bring your handcuffs to the reunion?

He looked down to his belt in surprise, as if he'd forgotten they were there. "'Cuz I couldn't bring my gun."

I sat back. "Wow. You made an adult decision and decided not to bring your gun. I'm impressed."

He looked at me through hooded eyes. "I didn't decide not to bring it. I couldn't bring it because I lost it." Kevin stared off into space. "Somewhere downtown, probably at the grocery store. Or in the park. I'm not sure."

And then he clambered down the bleachers and went back over to sit by Cindy. I didn't know which was worse…being trapped with a killer or being trapped with Kevin Dooley.

CHAPTER SIX

"Merry." Kelly motioned for me to come down, and I did.

"Did you find a flashlight?" I asked hopefully.

She shook her head. "We have another problem. The girls need to use the bathroom."

That *was* a problem. In my experience, when a child says they need to go, it really means they needed to go half an hour ago but ignored it until it was almost too late.

I ran over to the girls' locker room door and studied it. It wasn't like the bar frame doors. This door had a knob. If I could give it a good kick right where the door latched, I could possibly get it open.

The sight of the hinges made me wonder how this door opened. If it opened inward, away from me, I could kick it in. If the door opened outward, I could kick it all day, but it wouldn't budge. I pulled out the hairpin and began to work on the lock. This was a complicated lock. Why did they need something like that? This was a school. Not a fortress against a zombie apocalypse. Then I remembered what Mitch had said about this being a nuclear fallout shelter. I guess it kind of was a bunker.

Kelly let out a frustrated sigh. "I guess I should start looking for buckets to put backstage…"

"Argh!" I grumped, grasping the doorknob to shake it.

It turned in my hand. The door was unlocked.

Kelly and I looked at each other.

"I swear that door was locked," I said.

She nodded. "I know. Maybe you picked it successfully."

I shook my head. "Nope. The cylinders didn't click. I'm going in to clear it and see if the other door is locked."

The lights went on with the flip of a switch.

"Oh, hey!" I said over my shoulder to Kelly. "They totally renovated in here. Looks nice."

On my immediate left was a boxy maze of lockers. On my right was a series of hooks—some of which had towels dangling from them. Straight ahead on the right were toilet stalls, and on the left were the showers. The door to the hallway was in the left corner, and sinks lined the back wall.

I checked all the bathroom stalls and the showers. No one was in there. The lockers all had padlocks on them, so fat chance of someone being in there.

The door to the hallway was locked. I jiggled the knob, but it didn't help. Toilets flushed behind me. The girls were in, then. I sat down on a bench and stared into space. Why did the killer unlock the locker room entrance to the gym?

Was he back among us and realized we'd need to use the bathrooms? That seemed a little too generous for someone who'd killed two of my classmates and tried to kill me.

"I think it's a spree killer." Betty appeared, standing in front of me.

"A spree killer?"

The child sat down next to me. "Oh sure. Serial killers have a certain type, and they don't kill a bunch of random people at the same time. A spree killer starts and just keeps killing until he's busted or dies."

"How do you know that?" When I was in fourth grade, I was reading *Charlotte's Web* and *The Cricket in Times Square*. It appeared that Betty was reading an encyclopedia of murder.

"I'm doing research for…a…thing…" she evaded.

"Did the killer unlock the door?" Lucinda called from the doorway. "Or did you miss that it was unlocked the first time?"

I momentarily considered burning off all her hair again.

"I didn't miss it," I snapped. "It was locked, but now it isn't."

Cindy pushed past her. "But why? What's the point?"

I had no idea. "Why lock us all in here in the first place?"

Betty said, "To pick us off one by one, of course."

Cindy and Lucinda stared at the little girl.

"She may be right," I admitted. "Although, I wouldn't have put that so candidly."

"Oh," Betty said. "I almost forgot. The interviews are over. Want to know what we found out?"

Just then, Lauren, Caterina, and Ava wheeled the chalkboard through the doorway. How did they get it off the stage? They pushed it over to me as Betty took the pointer from the chalk tray.

It was impressive how they had managed a complete map of the gym. Sure, they took a few liberties with things, like Godzilla stomping Barry to death and Mothra circling the ceiling.

I squinted. "Is that Superman breaking a ninja janitor in half?"

Caterina nodded. "It's that Mitch guy. He's a hottie."

"Yeah," Lauren piped up. "Why did you break up with him?"

The four girls looked at me expectantly.

"I didn't break up with him because we never dated," I explained.

Ava shook her head. "That's not what he said."

Betty gave the other girls a look. "Denial is so sad in the elderly."

"Hey! I'm not elderly!" I complained. "And I'm not in denial either. Mitch never once spoke to me in high school. I swear."

"Yeah, right," Lauren scoffed.

I held out my pinky. "I pinky swear."

Four little girls gasped. The pinky swear was an unbreakable promise. More serious than wedding vows or nuclear treaties. With my troop, the pinky swear was the ultimate way to tell the truth or promise something.

The girls all hooked their pinkies around mine and nodded.

"Okay, Mrs. Wrath. We believe you," Lauren said.

"Why didn't you go for that guy?" Ava asked. "He's gorgeous!"

"I didn't say I didn't think he was cute," I confirmed. "I just said that he never had anything to do with me."

"Knock knock!" Mitch called from the doorway. "May I come in?"

"No, you're supposed to be watching your classmates," I said.

That's when I noticed that all the others were in the locker room. Mitch didn't move from the doorway.

"Everyone's fine." He walked in. "They're still unconscious. I just wanted to make sure you are alright." He winked.

Kelly looked from me to him and back again. "I just don't get it."

"Mitch," I explained. "Seriously. We never even acknowledged each other ten…"

"Eleven!" Cindy chimed in.

"Eleven," I corrected, "years ago. Why do you think we did?"

Mitch smiled but shook his head. "I know you're trying to save face in front of everyone. But there's really no point denying it."

Save face? If I'd dated Mitch Aiken, I'd make sure every single person remembered that.

"I'm not saving face. I'm happily married," I growled. Although I couldn't help but picture Rex being totally amused by this. There wasn't a jealous bone in his perfectly toned body.

"Just head back out there," I insisted.

"One question." He held up a finger. "The guys would like equal time for bathroom breaks. When the ladies are finished, that is."

I hadn't thought of that. "Okay. All the guys need to get out. When the last woman finishes, tell the guys they can have the room."

Mitch gave me the thumbs-up and blew me a kiss before retreating.

Kelly's hand reached out and grabbed the imaginary kiss. "What are you doing?" I asked.

She looked sheepish. "I couldn't just let it fall on the floor. That would be wrong."

"It's not real," I told her.

"It just seemed to be a waste," she mumbled.

With Mitch gone, I instructed the women to use the bathroom and reminded them to let the men know when they were done. I insisted that we keep the door propped open. That way we'd know if the killer tried to close and lock it again. Then I walked out into the gym, with the girls pushing the chalkboard behind me.

I sat down at a table, trying to make sense of all of this.

Kelly joined me. "What are we going to do?"

"Not a clue." I shrugged. "I guess the first priority would be to make sure no one else is killed. Which should be pretty easy since we are all trapped in here together."

I got up and flipped the chalkboard to the other side and began writing.

Kelly pointed. "First we have the ninja janitor locking us in here and no cell service."

"First," I corrected, "I think we should start with Marla's speech. That may have been the catalyst."

Kelly shook her head. "We don't know that. After all, you and Barry didn't make speeches."

I thought about this. "I think the attempt on me was a crime of opportunity. I'd discovered that Marla was murdered, and the killer didn't like that."

I wrote a list of victims, which I hoped would stay a short list. I put an asterisk by my name. Ava took a piece of chalk and wrote, *Almost dead but will probably die of old age in, like, the next year or so.*

"If we go with that," Kelly mused, "then we have the motive for Marla's murder, but not Barry's."

I thought about our conversation earlier. "Maybe Barry did see the killer?"

"He was doped up on LSD," Kelly pointed out.

"Perhaps the killer didn't know that or didn't want to count on that."

My best friend sighed. "If we follow that line of logic, then there shouldn't be any more murders. And yet, we are still locked in. Why not let us out?"

I tapped the chalk against my chin. The others had started to pull up chairs around us.

"If we're trapped in here until the middle of the night, why don't we start with just examining Marla's murder?" Lucinda asked.

"Step by step." I nodded. "Good idea, Lucinda."

The anchorwoman sat up a little straighter. I guess she had given up on being afraid of me. That was good. Besides, there wasn't a lighter or anything in here.

I erased the list of victims and wrote *Marla* in the upper, left hand corner. "Let's talk about the speech."

"Ugh," Cindy groaned. "Let's not."

There were a few titters of agreement.

"We have to. It might be the motive," Mitch said as he stood next to me.

I was pretty happy that the charm he had in high school had no effect on me now. Apparently, it did on Kelly, but not me.

I wrote *speech* under Marla's name. "She insulted pretty much everyone here."

Kelly piped up, "And suggested she had secrets to reveal later."

"Right!" I said. "We have to figure out if the killer murdered her because of the mean things she said or to silence her from revealing a secret."

Kevin raised his hand and asked, "Are we sure they're dead and not faking to get the special Seamus dessert?"

Judy spoke up. "How do we find out if she was killed for secrets?"

Betty stepped forward, punching her fist into her hand. "The Betty way."

"Who *are* these kids?" Mitch got behind me.

"My Girl Scout troop," I said. "And no, we aren't going to do it the Betty way."

To be honest, I wasn't sure what the Betty way actually was, but I was pretty sure I wouldn't like it. The kid was drugging adults with LSD, studying serial and spree killers, and was, well, Betty.

Betty sniffed. "We are junior detectives with the Who's There Police."

Kevin's eyes grew wide. "We have junior detectives? I'll never get promoted now."

Cindy looked at him. "You're a professional. They wouldn't promote kids before an experienced officer! Right, Merry?"

Oh, I had every bit of confidence to believe Betty would, if they had junior detectives, have outranked Kevin long ago.

"Girls," I warned. "We are all going to take part in this process like we do in troop meetings when decisions have to be made."

Well, we were going to do it like I *wish* decisions were made. Kelly and I always started out democratically, but it always ended with Betty hijacking things and the girls just going along with it. To be fair, she usually had the best, if not the most dangerous, ideas. Although lately, a lot of her ideas involved Basque separatists and kidnapping the mayor. I usually shot those down. Usually.

Kelly took over. "Does anyone remember exactly what Marla said?"

Judy looked at a pair of twins next to her. And I realized that I'd made no effort to figure out who the other people in our group were. Besides a set of pretty, blonde twins, there were three guys I didn't recognize.

It made me uncomfortable, not knowing who all the players were. As a spy, I'd often had to memorize the entire staff of an embassy, a prime minister's administration, a Yakuza mob boss's mob, and once—every member of the Russian Olympics curling team, including their lucky wombats. I'm talking about thirteen real, live marsupials. Did you know they poop cubes? See? I remembered *that* too.

In this case, however, these were my classmates. I'd gone to school with most of them from age five to age eighteen. I should know who they were, and I didn't. It was a bit embarrassing. Well, not like shouting at the Olympics Curling

Finals, "Holy cow, those wombats poop cubes!" embarrassing, but close.

Kelly read my mind like she usually does. "Hey, can we just take a minute and go around to give our names? I mean, of course we all know each other, but it would help since Merry's so bad at names."

I decided to go with it. "I am bad at names."

The twins did not seem offended and one of them spoke. "I'm Ashley, and this is Amanda. We were cheerleaders." She motioned to the bodies on the gym floor. "Along with others."

She pointed at the girl who'd been screaming about flying emus. From the fear on her sleeping face, I guessed she was still running from them. That was some powerful LSD. It didn't usually work in sleep. I needed to get some more intel from Betty. It could come in handy, especially if we could use it to make people crave Girl Scout cookies while they slept! Maybe we could make enough money to go to Costa Rica or Estonia!

"I'm Brandon." A guy my height with red hair and freckles stared directly into my eyes. "My locker was right next to yours in middle school and high school." He leaned back, folding his arms over his chest as if daring me to say I didn't remember him.

"Oh, right!" I said weakly. "Hi, Brandon! Nice to see you."

My mind was blank. I couldn't picture him as a teenager. His voice did sound a bit familiar though—which meant I did, sort of, remember him. I mean, obviously someone's locker was next to mine, so why couldn't it have been his?

Brandon wasn't buying it and scowled. I guess he was angry I hadn't acknowledged him yet. "We chatted *every* day."

"We did?" Now I really felt bad.

"Yeah," he insisted. "You'd ask me to stop blocking your locker, or is that the second bell, or you'd ask if it was raining. We were practically best friends."

I snapped my fingers. "I remember now. Sorry about that. It's nice to see you, Brandon."

I lied—hopefully convincingly. But since those seemed like the kind of things you'd say to someone whose locker was next to yours, I decided he must be right. He was definitely exaggerating about the best friends thing though. I would never have said those things to Kelly.

Brandon scoffed. He didn't seem to believe me. Man, I was losing my touch—first with my memory and secondly with my lying capabilities. I'd need to work on that.

"I'm Jason," said a very average looking guy. "I was in band and theater and didn't really hang out with any of you." He motioned to the floor. "But since my friends are all passed out, I'm hanging with you now."

Everyone else nodded like they knew who he was, so I did too. When in doubt, go along with the others. It's spycraft 101, and it works. People only notice if you stand out or go against the groupthink. Jason would've made a good spy. His looks were so generic with his brown hair, average height, and a face you'd forget five seconds after meeting. Lucky guy.

"And I'm Dylan," a moody dude said. "I was considered to be one of the druggies, so nothing ever came of my life."

Whoa. Way to saddle your graduating class with your problems.

Lucinda's eyes widened. "I remember you. You were always just off of school property, smoking. The principal tried to expel you, but since you weren't technically on the premises, he couldn't." She smiled with pride in remembering that.

"That's all you remember about me?" Dylan asked with an ugly sneer.

Lucinda's smile fell. "Of course not! You were an athlete too, right?"

Dylan shook his head.

"I know." Veronica thought she had it. "You took shop class every year!"

"Nope" was all he said.

"Chess club!" Kelly added.

"Not a chance!" he snapped.

Mitch cleared his throat. "What else did you do, Dylan? Help us out here."

Dylan threw up his arms. "Nothing! I didn't participate in anything! But you still should've remembered more about me than my smoking before school started." He began to sulk.

Kevin spoke slowly, like a slow-witted bear who'd just woken up from hibernation. "You ran the projector in class."

Dylan smiled, and we gasped. It obviously didn't come naturally to him, as it completely changed his face. "You're right, Kevin. I did do that."

There were murmurs of *Oh, right* and *I remember you now*, but I'm pretty sure everyone else was making that up. Betty came over and asked what a projector was, but I told her I'd tell her later.

"Okay," I said quickly. "Now that we all remember each other..."

Brandon rolled his eyes.

I ignored it. "Let's get back to the question. What did Marla say in her speech?"

"She insulted the football players, the cheerleaders, Kevin, and *you*." Veronica glared at me. "And you wished a two-ton weight would fall on Marla and kill her."

Every single head turned my way—except for Betty, who was sharpening chalk sticks on the edge of the blackboard, giving each one a deadly pointy tip.

Veronica fixed me with a steely glare. "And that's how she died, crushed by a weight!"

Apparently, my real estate agent didn't think I was hilarious anymore. She thought I was a killer. What worried me most was that some of my classmates might be thinking the same thing.

CHAPTER SEVEN

"I didn't kill her," I said calmly.

"I'll never be your real estate agent again," Veronica said grimly.

"Okay," I said. Weirdly, I missed when she laughed at everything I said. "But I didn't kill her. Marla was awful and was being very cruel. Tell me any of you didn't wish for that too."

Lucinda agreed. "I wanted her to get eaten by wolves."

"I hoped she'd get some disfiguring disease," Judy added.

"See?" I confirmed. "I'm not the only one."

Kevin raised his hand. "I was mad at her because she died, and now we can't have the Seamus dessert."

In a strange way, that took Kevin out of the list of suspects, which at this moment, included everyone in the room who was still standing. I knew Kevin, Kelly, the girls, and I did not kill Marla. And I was pretty sure Cindy didn't do it. I'd like to think Lucinda, Veronica, and Judy hadn't. But the others were a toss-up.

"It could've been any of us," Dylan snapped. "I think we should focus more on getting out of here."

Mitch nodded. "I vote for that. Let's get out first. I don't want to wait for the janitor."

Brandon, Jason, and the twins' heads bobbed in agreement.

"He's not wrong, Merry," Cindy said sheepishly. "Getting out of here does seem to be more important. I, for one, don't want to be trapped in here for hours with two corpses."

I waved toward the doors. "Be my guest. I've tried pushing, shoving, and picking the locks. If you guys can come up with something, I think that's a good idea."

And I meant it too. I had hoped that focusing on the murders wouldn't remind people that we were totally trapped here. But maybe giving them a problem to solve, like getting us out of here, would be better.

"I nominate Kevin to handle the investigation." Cindy beamed at the man who was staring at the food table. Sadly, all the food had been thrown at other people, and there wasn't much left but crumbs on napkins. "You can help him, Merry. The rest of us will work on the doors."

"You've done a great job, though," Judy said. "You've kept us all from panicking and all that."

"Thank you," I said.

Veronica continued to glare at me. Hopefully, she'd help the others.

The others, excluding Kelly, Kevin, and the girls, followed Mitch over to one of the doors. It was a relief. Trying to think with all those people pitching in with theories was exhausting.

"Do you think they'll find a way out?" Kelly asked.

"I can secretly infiltrate them," Betty said.

"They'll know it's you." Ava smoothed the front of her dress.

"I don't think it will work," I said gently. How did she think they wouldn't notice a tiny child in their midst?

Ava continued, "You're not wearing a name tag. That'll tip them off."

That will tip them off?

"I hope they get the doors open," I said. "I wouldn't mind the police tackling this one."

"Me too," Kevin said. "The police will do a way better job than us."

I shot him a look. "You're the police."

He looked around. "Who is?"

I tapped him on the shoulder. "You are."

"I'm what?" Kevin seemed genuinely confused. How did Rex work with him?

It wasn't worth the frustration. "Never mind. Why don't you go see if you can find out where Marla hid the Seamus treats?"

Happy to have a task involving food, Kevin loped away.

Mitch and the gang were poking at the doors. That's literally all they were doing.

It looked like Kelly was staring at the others, but I was pretty sure she was just watching Mitch. "Maybe we should help them."

I shook my head. "There's nothing to do. I don't think they're going to get the doors open. But giving them that as busy work helps us."

Her eyes turned back to me. "How?"

"Because now we can look at all the suspects." I pointed at the group, where Dylan was trying to unlock the doors with a credit card that promptly broke.

"That's our suspect pool?" Kelly asked skeptically.

"It's hard to imagine, right? Since it isn't one of us, it's probably one of them. After all, we haven't had another dead body since…" My voice broke off as I spotted Amanda sitting on the floor, back against the wall.

To the casual observer, she might've looked like she was resting. But something about the way she didn't blink tipped me off.

"Kelly!" I cried as I ran over to the twin.

Kelly beat me there and knelt down to check the twin's neck for a pulse. When she didn't get one, she laid Amanda flat on the floor and began administering CPR.

Ashley looked over and gasped, dropping to her knees beside her sister. "What can I do?" she begged Kelly.

But Kelly was in the nurse zone and working hard at it. She thought there was a chance to revive her. Mitch and Cindy stood protectively next to the girls, who'd joined us.

"We know CPR." Betty chafed at having a guard.

"And first aid too." Caterina's eyes were wide as she stared at the scene playing out in front of her.

I joined Ashley on the floor and scanned the body for any sign of trauma. There were no ligature marks. Not that I'd expected any because I'd hope these guys would've noticed if someone was strangling a woman right next to them. There were no wounds, no knives protruding from important places.

Had she had a stroke? A heart attack? It was possible. Could she have been poisoned? How was it managed with all of us right here? It didn't seem possible.

After five minutes, Kelly finally stopped. She looked at Ashley and shook her head. "I'm so sorry."

Ashley was stunned. She looked at me. "Can't you do something?"

I put my arm around her. "Kelly was an emergency room nurse. If she can't help, there's nothing I can do. Ashley, I'm so sorry."

Ashley got to her feet, took off her long kimono, and draped it over her sister. Then she flung herself into a very surprised Dylan's arms and sobbed.

Kelly held up three fingers. I nodded. Betty gave me a knowing look. She was right. We were dealing with a spree killer.

CHAPTER EIGHT

Dylan awkwardly guided a sobbing Ashley to the bleachers, and she was glued to him. The others joined them, surrounding Ashley and offering sympathy, while Kelly, the girls, and I stayed where we were. It was awful. No one minded that Marla was killed, and people were a bit sad when Barry was murdered. But Ashley lost her sister. Her twin!

"I think she was poisoned," Kelly murmured. "And the effect was instantaneous. But we won't know for sure without an autopsy."

"Bludgeoning, strangulation, and now poisoning." I shook my head. "And we are trapped in here with the killer with no way to call for help."

"We have to get the girls out of here," Kelly said.

Lauren heard that and stomped her foot. "We aren't going anywhere."

"Yeah!" Ava stuck out her chin. "We can help you."

Caterina quietly agreed as Betty began putting the sharpened chalk sticks between her fingers like Wolverine.

"I don't think the killer will go after them." I tapped my chin. "I think this has to do with our classmates."

"You're saying the killer had special reason to kill Marla, Barry, and Amanda?" Kelly stared at me. "Those three had nothing in common."

"They were all popular," I said. "Marla made fun of the football team, which Barry was part of, and the cheerleaders, which Amanda was part of."

"Do you think the killer is picking off the people in Marla's speech?" Kelly asked. "Because if so, you're on the hit list too."

I nodded. "So's Cindy, Mitch, Kevin, and Lucinda. You, however, are safe. I wonder why she didn't call you out."

Kelly shrugged. "There's nothing to say. I never crossed her in high school."

I was going to suggest it didn't matter when she continued.

"Besides, she didn't name everyone here. She didn't mention Brandon, Jason, or Dylan." She swept her arm over the prone bodies. "Or most of them."

"That's true," I agreed. "It would've been a long speech if she had. And the way she was going, someone probably would've killed her right in front of us just to shut her up."

I heard whispering and turned to see the girls in a tight huddle.

"You guys okay?" Kelly asked.

Lauren spoke for the group. "I think we saw the killer."

Okay, that got our full attention. Kelly and I joined the huddle.

"What did you see?" I asked in a hushed tone.

Caterina, Ava, and Betty looked at Lauren and nodded.

"Well," the tall redhead said slowly, "they were all pushing at the doors. The dead girl was talking to her sister and that Mitch guy. Then Mitch was swinging his arms around while he talked, and he accidentally hit the dead girl with the back of his hand."

"Boy, did she look mad," Caterina added.

"It wasn't much of a hit," Betty said. "She really overreacted to it like she was in pain. She should've started a fight club."

I had to ask. "A fight club?"

Betty studied me. "It's where you learn how to take a punch. We're thinking of starting one."

"No fight clubs," Kelly declared.

"At least not until you're eighteen," I added.

Kelly gave me a sharp look.

"I mean never," I corrected.

Lauren continued, "And then the dead girl kind of sat down. She hasn't moved since."

I got down on her level. "Where did he hit her?"

Lauren pointed to her own upper left arm. "She grabbed her arm when it happened."

I turned to Kelly. "We need to check it out."

My best friend shook her head. "A minor slap in the arm with the back of a hand isn't enough to kill someone."

She was wrong about that. "In 1978, the KGB killed a Bulgarian dissident named Markov. They passed him on the street and touched him with the tip of their umbrella, which embedded a pellet full of ricin." Out of the corner of my eye I saw Betty get out her notebook.

"Spell ricin," she asked. "And do you have an umbrella like that?"

Lauren thought for a second. "We could maybe order it on Amazon."

"You." I pointed to Betty. "Are not ordering a lethal umbrella on Amazon using my credit card."

Kelly elbowed me.

"You," I repeated. "Are not ordering a lethal umbrella on Amazon. And no, I don't have one."

This was technically true. I didn't have a killer umbrella. But I did have a cat collar that fired a deadly laser, a tampon box that doubled as an Uzi, and chloroform wipes. But no umbrella. Thank God.

I bent over Amanda's body. Kelly and the girls joined me and watched.

"Her left arm," Lauren reminded me.

I looked around. The others were all still huddled around Ashley. I lifted the jacket and rolled up her sleeve. There was a bruise, but no puncture wound. I rolled the sleeve back down, got up, and stepped away.

"No wound. I don't think Mitch killed her. At least, not that way." Now, why didn't I feel relieved? Was it because he was my imaginary boyfriend? Well, imaginary boyfriend or no, I needed to look at all suspects with a clear, impartial mind.

Kelly wondered, "Had she eaten something just before?"

Betty shook her head. "No. But she did squirt some spray up her nose. It's like the stuff my brother uses for his allergies."

Kelly and I looked at each other, but this time, she waved me off and went over to the body. We watched as she searched the body—purse, pockets, and all. Finally, she got up and rejoined us.

"There's no inhaler on her, in her purse, or near the body." She told us what we had already guessed.

"The killer took it," I said grimly. "Which means that they knew Amanda used an inhaler and switched it out so that she'd use the poisoned one."

Kelly saw where I was going. "Which means the killer knew her well enough to do that. Could that narrow the field?"

"More than with Marla or Barry," I decided. "And we know it had to be someone in that group. Which also narrows it down." I looked around. "Which reminds me, what happened to Kevin?"

The others looked around too. But Officer Kevin Dooley was nowhere to be found.

"You." I pointed at Kelly. "Take the girls and check the locker room. I'll check backstage."

We split up and moved quietly so as not to draw the attention of the others, who were still soothing Ashley. Good. I didn't want them following us. One of them was a killer, and until I knew who, it was better to stay away from them.

Up on the stage, I searched the left side and then the right. Marla was still there, but no Kevin. Where could he have gotten off to? My heart skipped a beat. Was he another victim? As annoying as the man was, I felt protective of him. He may be the village idiot—but he was *our* village idiot.

"Kevin!" I called out. "Where are you?"

"Mmmgorf..." came the reply.

It sounded like he was tied up and gagged. Behind the main backdrop, I saw his legs sticking out from behind a large wooden house prop.

"Kevin!" I raced over, only to find he was not tied up and gagged.

His mouth was full of cake. Cupcakes, in fact. On the floor, between his knees, was a large box with several dozen cupcakes. They'd been decorated with little tombstones that had *RIP* written in frosting. Classy, Marla. Real classy.

I picked up the box and found the lid. "This is for everyone," I chastised.

Kevin swallowed. "I was hungry."

He got to his feet and brushed away a significant amount of crumbs. "Did I miss something?"

"Amanda was murdered. Poisoned, we think." I looked at the box of cupcakes. "Where did you find these? I don't remember seeing them backstage."

Kevin pointed to the floor. There was a ring and the outline of a trapdoor.

How had I missed that? "You went down there?"

He thought about it for a moment. "Yes. Yes, I definitely went down there. And found the cupcakes."

"Is there a way out of here?" I felt like I was questioning a toddler about something he didn't want to tell.

Kevin shrugged.

Against my better judgement, I handed him the box of cupcakes. "Don't eat these. I'm going down there."

"Okay," he said.

I pulled the ring, and the trap door opened easily. Lights came on below, revealing a set of stairs. Either they were motion sensitive, or someone was down there. I stepped down onto the first step and then continued to the bottom.

The room was filled with makeup tables and racks of costumes. This was the dressing room. How did I not know this was here? Not that I'd been involved with drama in school. But it seems that it would have come up. At the very least, Jason might have mentioned it since he'd done theater here.

Looking around the room, I didn't see any doors. But I did see a table with a purse on it. Could it be Marla's? It had to be since this was where Kevin had found the cupcakes. Before even attempting to touch it, I pulled a pair of arm-length white gloves off of a nearby costume and slipped them on.

It was a Prada designer bag. I unsnapped the closure and opened it up. Inside was a Gucci wallet. I took it out and looked through it. There was Marla's driver's license. There were some credit cards and money. I searched every crevice and pulled out a folded piece of paper, which I opened and read.

It was a letter from Hanson, Evers & Trollope Stock Brokerage. Marla had been fired a few weeks ago. The reason for the firing was embezzlement. The firm thanked her for repaying the money and agreed not to press charges. They were probably happy just cutting her loose.

Wasn't this interesting? Not only had she been fired, but she carried the letter around in her purse. I felt a twinge of smugness that I immediately felt bad for. I put the letter back and continued going through the purse.

There wasn't much in there besides keys, expensive makeup, and something cylindrical. My fingers closed around it, and I pulled it out. It was an inhaler. The kind used for sinus congestion.

Was it Amanda's?

I put it back in the purse and slung the bag over my shoulder. Back onstage, I took the cupcakes from Kevin and led him back to the gym floor, where we deposited the purse and cupcakes on the table where we'd been sitting. Kelly spotted me and came over.

"You found all that? Where?" Kelly asked. "Why are you wearing opera gloves?"

I explained through a mouthful of cupcake. What? I was hungry too. Kevin had followed me back and was angling for another cupcake, but I held him off.

"If it is the poisoned inhaler," Kelly reasoned, "that means the killer put it in Marla's purse."

I thought so too. "Did we see anyone slip away from the crowd to go backstage?"

"Officer Dooley would've seen them," Betty said. "He was there, right?"

Ava looked at it. "Then maybe it isn't the right inhaler."

Betty reached for it. "We should try it out." She looked at the passed out bodies on the floor. "Which one do you like the least?"

I pulled it out of her reach. "We aren't doing that. But I do have an idea."

CHAPTER NINE

"Yes," Ashley said through her tears. "That's hers. Amanda always had a bottle of it on her. Why?"

We were all sitting around the table, with the girls standing behind Kelly and me, attempting to look menacing.

"We didn't find a bottle on her," Kelly said gently.

"But that's impossible. I know it was in her purse." Ashley frowned. "Wait, you don't think this killed her, do you?"

Kelly explained that she didn't see any other way except for the possibility of natural causes.

Ashley shook her head violently. "She wasn't poisoned! No one would kill her! Maybe she had an aneurism or something!"

Dylan seemed alarmed that she was agitated and began patting her back. He was really concerned for her, maybe because it was the first time that a pretty woman had flung herself into his arms.

I looked around the table at each and every one of them. "As soon as we get out of here, there'll be an autopsy, and we will know for sure."

Amanda's twin seemed awfully convinced that her sister had died from natural causes. Ashley knew her sister used the sinus spray. Would she have killed her?

"Kevin!" Cindy cried out. "What do we do?"

Kevin looked like he was going to shrug. Instead, he said, "We have to find a way out. First priority. Then we send a few people to the police station for help and to call the hospital while the rest of us stay here to stand guard."

No one spoke as all eyes were on Kevin.

He let out a breath and kind of deflated. Then he took a cupcake, looked at me, and asked, "What was the question?"

"You just answered it." Betty studied him like a slug who'd just developed the ability to sing opera.

"I did?" Kevin looked at Cindy, who nodded.

"Yeah," Lauren added. "And it was a good answer."

He scratched his head. "Oh. Then we should do whatever I said."

Cindy didn't seem fazed at all. "It's a great plan. Now, how do we get out of here?"

Mitch put his hand over mine. "I'll stay here with the women."

I yanked my hand out from under his. "The women are fine. I can handle things without you."

Mitch looked visibly wounded. I needed to take him aside and have a little chat with him about this.

"I'll go," Cindy offered. "And Judy can come with me."

That was more like it.

"I'll go too," Brandon said. No one paid him any attention.

"I'll stay here with Amanda," Ashley said with a catch in her voice.

"And I'll stay with Ashley." Dylan put his arm around her, and she leaned against him. The look on his face was one you might see on someone who'd won the lottery and couldn't believe it. I didn't really remember him, but it was obvious the two hadn't moved in the same circles in high school.

"Alright." I stood up. "We're going to do it this time. Let's figure out how to get you guys out of here." Who knows? Maybe Kevin will have another one of…whatever that was…and come up with a brilliant idea.

This time I went to the locker room, straight through to the door to the hallway. The lock was old. Solid. It had had to stand up to years of kids trying to break in to smoke, mess around, and so on.

Kids, even back then, had some ingenuity. And if they couldn't get through, maybe I couldn't. But it was the one lock we hadn't tried.

"Stand back!" Mitch said, parting us like the Red Sea. "I'll handle this!"

"Mitch," I started.

"Don't worry, Merry." He put his finger on my lips. "I can do this."

I took that finger and twisted it to the side. He didn't even cry out, which was kind of admirable. I let go.

"You may have been a spy." He shook his hand out. "But I have something better. I played high school football." He took off his jacket and undid the top two buttons of his shirt before handing the jacket to me.

"Mitch!" I shouted.

Before I could warn him, he ran for the door, slamming his body against it. It didn't budge. Mitch cried out in pain, nursing his shoulder.

"It opens inward," I said. "You can't bust out."

He limped over, his face a mask of pain. "Can you look at my shoulder? I think I dislocated it."

I pushed him over to Kelly and bent down once more to inspect the lock. From the cry I heard behind me, Kelly must've reset Mitch's shoulder.

Seriously? What was with this guy? His ego was large enough to claim he'd been romantically involved with me when he hadn't. That alone was enough for me to want to teach him a lesson.

Quite a few men at the CIA were like that. Even with more women in the ranks who were every bit as (if not much more) intelligent than they were, they never failed to stoop to imply that they'd "showed the woman around The Farm."

During my training, there was this guy named Mark, who thought he was God's gift to women. For weeks, he'd bragged to the other men about bagging one woman after another. Most of the women ignored him. Except for Selena.

Selena was a petite and pretty farm girl from Kansas. She showed bulls, tossed hay bales and, what Mark didn't know, was the first woman wrestler in Kansas high school history. So when Mark said he'd bedded her, I sat back and watched.

Selena threw him through a door, where he landed facedown on a table just before she broke a chair over his back.

Mark quit the minute he got out of the hospital, moved back to Florida, and became one of those ubiquitous "Florida Men" you see on the news for doing something stupid. He'd tried to hold up a convenience store with an alligator. A real, living one. Not only did he fail at the robbery attempt and make the national news, he also lost three fingers to the alligator, who now lives in a children's zoo.

Selena went on to a field assignment in Eastern Europe, where she spies undercover as a professional wrestler and chicken juggler. Based on how much time I'd spent in Chechnya, I'd be willing to bet that she's very popular there.

Betty appeared at my shoulder. "Do you need a pick?"

I shook my head. "I don't think it would work." I got to my feet to think. We'd tried everything I could think of. "We know the janitor can let us out at two."

"I don't think we should stay here one moment more," Kelly said quietly. "With three bodies, this killer is proving he may not stop there." Kelly suggested that they split into groups, each group taking an exit.

"With you observing," I insisted.

Kelly pointed to the gym. "I'll be standing in the middle of the gym and watching everything."

Everyone filed out. Everyone, that is, but Betty.

I slumped onto the bench and sighed. "We're getting nowhere."

Betty sat next to me, also sighing. "And there are lots of dead people."

"We're fine," I said as convincingly as possible.

"I'm not worried," Betty said. "Whoever this killer is, he's after adults. You are more in danger than we are."

She was probably right. "That's true."

Betty scratched her ear. "So who do you think did it?"

I looked at her. "Who do *you* think did it?"

"I think it's a dude," Betty said. "That Mitch hottie or the redhead or the weird guy who looks like any other guy or the creeper."

I'd been thinking the same thing. "Can you be more specific?"

"The redhead is obvious." Betty rolled her eyes. "He's the dude who's mad because no one remembers him."

"Brandon," I said.

Betty took out her little notebook and wrote that down. "Brandon. Right. And the average guy whose friends are supposedly lying on the floor and said he was in a band."

"That's Jason," I said. "He took band when he was here—and theater. Which must mean that the creeper is Dylan."

Betty scribbled the names down. "If I had to narrow it down, I'd say it's Jason or Brandon."

It was then I realized she had the little chalk spikes she'd made sticking out of the top of her sash. That was good thinking—stashing the weapons for later. This girl was destined to be a spy. She knew you could make ordinary things around her into weaponry. I've seen her lick lollipops into shivs, break bottles into jagged weapons, and one time at camp, she used a flaming marshmallow to terrorize an older girl who'd been picking on Caterina. Sorry. I can't tell you that story because of the unbreakable pinky swear. But it's a good one, I can tell you that.

One story I can tell you is that, in the Cold War, OSS spies were taught how to roll a newspaper into a sharp object that could puncture skin—but they'd stopped doing that in the 90s because they just assumed everyone had a gun all the time. I'd always liked that story. I could've used that training once when I was being chased through a newspaper printing facility in Caracas by a Venezuelan drug lord who was dressed as Ethel Merman.

Why was Three Bullets Batista dressed like Ethel Merman? I never got the chance to ask because Riley caught up to me and took him out. I never did forgive him for that one. I had tried to ask one of Batista's flunkies once during an interrogation, but he clammed up.

Why was he called Three Bullets? Because he had terrible aim, and it usually took three tries before he actually hit something. And that was on a good day. Half the time he'd empty his magazine without hitting anything. Which was another reason I was mad at Riley. I probably could've charged "Ethel" with a strong chance of not getting hit. But nooooo. Riley had to shoot him.

Why were we in a newspaper printing facility? You know what? I don't remember. But that rolled-up newspaper trick would've come in handy.

"Why do you suspect Brandon and Jason?" I asked.

"Because nobody remembers them," Betty said. "I know all the kids in my grade. I have a board with all their pictures on a wall in my bedroom, with information about each one. Someday that's gonna come in handy, no matter what my parents think."

I stared at her as it hit me. "You're right! Brandon complains over and over that he's upset that we don't recognize him! What if he's saying that because he actually wasn't part of the class!"

"And that Jason dude said he didn't hang out with any of you, just the people on the floor," Betty said. "So who knows if he really went to school with you?"

"It's possible that both, or at least one, of them wasn't in our class!" I nodded. "But wait, why would they want to murder people they didn't even go to school with?"

"Spree killer," Betty said.

"What about Dylan? He's also on your list. But I kind of vaguely remember someone like him," I said.

"Because he's creepy," Betty said. "Duh."

"That's not enough to convict someone of murder," I chided.

Betty stood up, smacking her fist into her palm. "Want me to torture them into squealing?"

A thought popped into my head. "Maybe later. Right now I've got a better idea."

CHAPTER TEN

I agreed with Kevin, for once in my entire life. Getting out of here was the best bet. But we also needed to know who the killer was so that we could tie him up until the authorities arrived. The idea that Brandon or Jason might be killers who'd intruded on our reunion had merit.

The only problem was motive. If they were outsiders, why kill certain people? Betty's idea about them being spree killers was interesting. It was a good opportunity for someone like that. An event with fifty-some folks in one room could be tempting to them.

And convincing a group of people that you're a long-lost classmate would be easy if they were under stress, like from having to go to your class reunion—or being picked off by a killer. Why hadn't I thought of that earlier? Betty was smart. And terrifying. But mostly smart.

We headed out to the gym. Kelly was standing in the center with Ava, Lauren, and Caterina, her eyes roving over the groups at the other locker room door and the main entrance. We sidled up to her and told her what we'd come up with.

Kelly frowned but kept studying the groups. "I don't know. Brandon and Jason could've been classmates. It's possible that we didn't really know them."

"Or." I held up my index finger. "It's possible that one of them isn't who they say they are."

"Yes," my best friend said. "But what's the motive?"

Betty nudged me. I shared her theory first. "It could be a spree killer. Or could it be that they were here to kill one person and are using the other murders to muddy the waters?"

Betty added, "My vote is spree killer. Too bad the killer didn't drink the punch. Then we'd be at Mrs. Albers' place right now, partying."

Lauren whooped. "I've got six jars of blackberry jam in my bag in the lobby just for that!"

Betty grilled the other two. "Did you guys bring the stuff you were supposed to?"

Ava nodded. "I've got the inflatable kiddie pool and rope."

Caterina added, "And I brought the Ouija board and cat shampoo!"

"Mrs. Albers doesn't have a cat," I said.

The four turned to me in unison. "What does that have to do with it?" they asked in perfect sync.

They really had to stop doing that. As for the weird crap they brought for a sleepover at Kelly's? That was her problem because now I sure as hell wasn't going to join them.

Kelly shuddered. "Back to the subject of our suspects. How do we find out if Jason or Brandon are imposters?"

"I've got an idea. Betty, you stay here with Mrs. Albers. I've got some questioning to do."

"Oh, no you don't." The kid put her hands on her hips. "I want in. I can be the heavy."

"I really would prefer that the girls don't antagonize the killer," Kelly said firmly.

I pointed at my co-leader. "You heard her. Stay here."

I approached the group at the boys' locker room first. Neither man was in this group—it was Cindy, Judy, and Kevin. At the main doors, Jason was with Lucinda, Veronica, and Dylan, while Brandon was commiserating with Mitch and Ashley not too far away.

"How's it going?" I asked.

Kevin frowned at the door. "I wish I'd brought my gun. I could've blown the lock off."

It was good that he hadn't brought his gun. Three Bullets Batista was a better shot than Officer Kevin Dooley.

"No luck," Cindy said. "You?"

"No," I admitted. "Hey, question…Brandon is really mad at me. He keeps saying I should know him because we were in classes together and his locker was next to mine, but I don't remember him."

Judy and Cindy looked across the gym at the redhead.

"He looks familiar," Judy said with a hint of doubt. "I'm sure there was a redheaded guy in our class, but I can't remember much about him."

Cindy squinted. "I was so low on the social totem pole that I really only remember the mean girls. Like Marla."

Judy nodded. "Everyone hated Marla. Everyone probably wanted her dead at one time or another."

Cindy put her hand on my arm. "Veronica's wrong. I know you didn't kill Marla."

Judy agreed. "That's right. If you had, why would you have worked so hard to find out if it was murder? You'd have declared it an accident, and we wouldn't have known better."

Awww, that's nice. They were on my side.

"What do you want us to do?" Cindy asked.

"Yeah," Judy said. "How can we help? I'm bored out of my mind right now."

I decided to trust them and told them to follow my lead.

We walked over to Brandon, Mitch, and Ashley, who were having no luck. Mitch was holding his sore shoulder. He wouldn't be flinging himself against any other doors tonight. Ashley was quiet and subdued, with quick glances every now and then to her sister's body. Dylan wasn't with her, which seemed a little odd, but maybe his charms wore off after she was done sobbing on his shoulder.

"How's it going?" Cindy asked.

Mitch brightened when he saw me. "Merry, my shoulder is killing me. Can you give me a massage?"

"No," I said. And not because I didn't have a special massage—I did. But it involved pain and was usually done when torturing someone. Tempting as it would be to do that to Mitch, we didn't have time for me to enjoy his pain.

"This is a bust," Brandon grumbled. "We've looked at these doors all night and haven't had one new idea."

"That sucks," Judy said. "This isn't much of a reunion, huh?"

Mitch came over and stood next to me. "I don't know. It has its perks."

I took into account that the man was injured and resisted the urge to drop him.

Ashley shook her head but said nothing.

"I shouldn't have come at all," Brandon groused. "Nobody remembers me, the prom queen is dead, like two others are, and we're trapped here." He threw his hands in the air. "Trapped here with no one who remembers me!"

"Sorry about that," I said as sympathetically as possible. "I remember you. Didn't we have gym together senior year?"

Brandon eyed me suspiciously and nodded.

Judy laughed. "I couldn't stand the gym teacher."

"Yeah, she was horrid." Cindy made a face. "What was her name again?"

We watched Brandon, who shrugged. The answer was Mrs. Spoletto.

"I hated gym," Brandon said. "All those idiot gym teachers blur into one big bully."

"Mrs. Spoletto," Ashley said quietly. "She was Amanda's favorite teacher."

Mitch cocked his head to one side. "She wasn't half bad. If you were a jock."

Brandon hadn't named Mrs. Spoleto, but that didn't mean he wasn't in our gym class. It wasn't exactly damning evidence.

"Do you guys remember the chemistry teacher?" Cindy said. "I got straight Cs in that class. The teacher never cut me any slack."

"Vaguely." Judy played along. "It wasn't my favorite subject either."

Mitch said, "I didn't take chemistry. Did you, Ashley?"

Ashley shook her head. Now we were cooking.

I snapped my fingers. "That's it! You were my lab partner," I said to Brandon. I said it quietly so that Lucinda wouldn't hear and have flashbacks.

Brandon shook his head. "No, I don't think so."

"Maybe it was physics, then," I persisted.

"Oh, yeah," he said weakly. "I think that's right."

I didn't take physics. At least, not one with a lab. But how to get him to trip up? I wasn't ready to accuse him outright. It wasn't exactly an open-and-shut case. People got things wrong about the past sometimes.

Mitch smiled. "I guess I should've taken those classes so that I could have been your lab partner, Merry."

I ignored him completely.

"What did you do after graduation, Brandon?" I tried to sound like someone who's embarrassed that they don't remember a classmate and tries to make up for it by being overly interested in what happened after.

"I went to college. Majored in business. Became an accountant. I work in Chicago," he said.

"Which college?" Cindy batted her eyelashes at him to appear flirty.

Brandon was unaffected. "University of Iowa."

That was an easy call. Most kids either went to Iowa, Iowa State or, if you were weird, the University of Northern Iowa. It's interesting that he chose the University of Iowa because I went to Iowa too, at the same time. But then, so did twenty thousand other kids. I majored in international studies. I was never around any business majors. Still, it seemed a half-strike against him since I knew a couple of other classmates who went to Iowa with me. It seems to me that I should've known if he'd been there.

Cindy talked about her new life in Kansas City. Ashley said she worked at the mall in Des Moines with her sister. She didn't say anything else. I felt pretty bad that her sister was out in the open. I'd move her, but it wasn't worth the flack I'd get from my husband.

"I went to Iowa State," Judy volunteered. "I'm the VP of Marketing at an insurance company in Des Moines."

I needed to get her and Ava together. I looked over at the girls and was surprised to see Kevin sitting with them at a table. Were they painting his nails? I squinted. Sure enough, they were. Kevin just stared into space as Caterina did his left hand in gold while Lauren painted the nails on his right hand in purple. Where'd they get the nail polish? I wanted to ask, but I was busy running an interrogation that didn't look like an interrogation. I turned back to the group.

"What about you, Mitch?" I asked to keep the cover going.

"Contracting," he said. "I started with my uncle's company in Waterloo and, in five years, made partner. We have offices in Davenport and Council Bluffs."

That sounded kind of impressive. It also explained how he knew that the gym was outfitted like a bunker.

"And you were a spy." Mitch wiggled his eyebrows. "A secret agent. How fascinating!"

I did not want this to be about me. It was time to change the subject. "Why don't you guys take a break, eat a cupcake if there are any left. Just don't drink the punch."

They agreed eagerly. When the others left, Judy asked, "Want us to go with you to interrogate Jason?"

"I'd rather you kept at it with Brandon," I whispered. "Maybe you guys can get more out of him. He still seems to be mad at me."

Cindy and Judy gave me a nod and joined the others.

"Hey, guys!" I joined Jason, Lucinda, Veronica, and Dylan.

"How's it going?" I asked.

Veronica narrowed her eyes and said nothing.

"No luck," Lucinda said. "We can't come up with any ideas."

"Too bad we don't have a sledgehammer." Jason looked at the walls. "Probably wouldn't work anyway."

Dylan sneered, his eyes on Ashley. "Well, we don't, and this is pointless. I'm going to see how Ashley is doing." And with that he wandered away.

"This is terrifying," Lucinda said. "We're trapped in here with a killer."

Veronica nodded, never taking her eyes off of me. I was tempted to argue the point with her, but I needed intel from Jason.

"This is awful with three people dead. We'll just have to wait for the janitor, I guess."

"Great," Veronica said sarcastically.

"Since we're here, we can chat a little to pass the time," I said with a small smile, not wanting to overdo it. "I don't feel like I've been able to catch up with you guys."

"I was your real estate agent," Veronica snapped. "There. Happy?" Then she stormed off toward the others.

Lucinda patted me on the back. "She really thinks you're the killer, Merry. That's all she's been talking about."

I guess I needed a new real estate agent. Not that I was moving anytime soon.

"Well, I know what you do, Lucinda. I see you every night on the news," I gushed.

She brightened. "Really? You watch?"

I nodded. "Every night. You do a good job too." I waited a beat. "Sorry about what happened in chemistry." I touched my hair.

She waved me off. "It's in the past. I was kind of a bitch back then. I probably deserved it."

That seemed like a bit of a breakthrough. Maybe I was on a lucky streak! I turned to Jason.

I chewed my lip. "I don't think we had the same classes, Jason."

He laughed. "I was in all AP classes when I wasn't in the band room or backstage here." He motioned to the stage.

Was he insulting me by saying I obviously wasn't smart enough to take advanced placement classes? I shoved that thought aside as another took its place.

"That's right," I said. "How come you didn't tell us about the dressing room under the stage?"

For a split second—if I'd blinked, I'd have missed it—Jason froze. It only lasted the briefest moment. Good thing I didn't blink often. In fact, I usually won staring contests with the girls. Three-time troop champion!

"I didn't think it was relevant," he said at last. "There isn't any way out from there."

That was true. Was he bluffing? Or had I said that when I brought out Marla's purse? I couldn't remember. So much for my excellent memory. I tried something else.

"This is kind of a bummer." I waved at the people sleeping soundlessly on the floor. "The people you know here are all passed out."

He cracked a disarming grin. "Yeah. I wasn't on the popular kids' radar. Or Marla might've had something in her tragic speech about me."

That's true. Marla hadn't mentioned Brandon either.

I tapped my chin. "I think I went to the musical senior year, but I can't for the life of me remember what it was. You must've been in that, and I didn't even realize it."

Jason didn't miss a beat. "I was usually in the chorus. I never made lead."

That was a good, safe answer.

"I remember that show!" Lucinda interjected. "It was *Oklahoma!* I was the lead." She turned and frowned a little. "I don't remember you from that, Jason."

He waved us off with a smile. "Why would you? You were the lead, and I was in the background."

Another good answer. And yet my spydy senses were tingling.

Lucinda shrugged. "Well, it was the first and only play I did here. I thought it might help with my career."

"That must be it," Jason said. "I remember you in *Oklahoma!*, but not in anything else."

"What have you been doing since high school?" Lucinda asked. I loved it because now the conversation had become organic. It wouldn't be suspicious.

Jason shrugged. "College. I live in Chicago now." He didn't say anything else.

I asked, "Do you and Brandon hang out? Did you come together?"

He frowned. "Brandon lives in Chicago? I guess I didn't know that. Well, it's a huge city and all."

Hmmm...Jason and Brandon had been hanging out all night together ever since our classmates took a nosedive into la-la land. Why wouldn't where they live have come up?

Lucinda cocked her head to one side. "Are you in theater there?"

He laughed. "No such luck. My degree is in theater and English. I work as a technical writer for a company that makes refrigerators. Boring, I know."

If he was lying, he was very good at it. As a spy, you have a cover where you tell people you do something dull so that you don't pique their interest—like being a tech writer for a refrigerator company. Who'd ask about that? Well, besides me, because I love refrigerators. That's where the food is.

"So, Merry, what about you? What have you been up to?" Jason asked a little too quickly.

"Haven't you heard the rumors?" Lucinda asked. "She was in the CIA."

Either Jason hadn't heard the rumors or had really infiltrated our reunion blind. He seemed surprised.

His eyebrows went up. "Really?"

I waited for him to say something about how he thought that was fitting due to some memory of me in high school. He didn't.

"That's right," I said. "I tried to keep it secret for a few years, but my past caught up with me."

"You were outed by the Vice President, right? I almost forgot," Lucinda said. "Can I interview you if we all make it out of here alive?"

"I don't think that would be a good idea," I said. "But thanks for the offer."

Jason pressed on. "Were you a field agent?"

It seemed safer to say I'd held a desk down, but then again, my ego wanted to say what I had really done. Don't most people want to go to their class reunion with a really cool story? Being a former spy at an event like this should be a dream come true.

However, most dreams weren't classified like my former life was. "I don't really want to go into it."

"Have you killed people?" Jason's eyes burned brightly. "Spies kill people! That would make you a main suspect here! Especially since Marla called you out."

I waved my hands in front of me, palms out. "I didn't kill Marla."

"The question is," Jason continued as if I hadn't said anything, "why did you kill Barry and Amanda?"

"I didn't." I narrowed my eyes. "I didn't kill anyone."

Jason turned to Lucinda. "She's at the top of my list now." And the two walked away.

His list? He has a list? He doesn't get to have a list! I'm the one with the list! For a second, I was impressed. He'd taken the interrogation and turned it away from himself, shining the spotlight on me instead. And it had been almost seamless. It didn't seem like a skill for a refrigerator tech writer. It seemed like a great skill for a spy.

I replayed the conversation in my mind as I joined the others, who'd all crowded around a table. I hadn't learned anything about Jason. And Brandon hadn't fallen into my trap. Was I losing my touch?

Betty walked around offering cupcakes, and Lauren offered punch. No one took her up on the punch. There were also several unopened bottles of beer and wine on the table. But no one seemed interested in drinking anything, in case it was all spiked.

"Nice manicure," I said to Kevin. "I like how you used the school colors."

Kevin looked at me quizzically, then at his hands. "Huh. When did that happen?"

Cindy gushed, "I love it! It takes a real man to let little girls paint your fingernails!"

Kevin looked at her blankly then said, "Okay."

I took an unopened beer bottle and turned it in my hands. "What happened to the bartender?"

Everyone looked around, which seemed silly since we'd know if the bartender were still here.

"She's over there." Lauren pointed to a prone woman on the floor. "I guess she drank the wrong thing." She held up a pitcher. "Punch, anyone?"

Cindy shook her head. "No, thank you. But I think it's very sweet how you girls are helping out."

"Aren't you a little scared?" Ashley asked as she started tearing up. Dylan put his arm around her shoulders.

"Nope." Betty set the remaining cupcakes on the table.

"But there's a killer on the loose in this gym!" Ashley started to tremble. "And you're probably serving them cupcakes!"

Betty blinked. "Lady, the only thing I'm scared of are grizzly bears, those who want to oppress the Basque people, and talking chickens."

It was a good list. I'd be afraid of those things too—if I were in the woods in Spain during bear breeding season, being chased by talking chickens. Who wouldn't?

"Yes, sweetie," Cindy said. "But there are no bears here or Spaniards, and talking chickens can't strangle or poison you."

Betty shrugged. "If the killer tries to kill me, I'll hit him in the head with a rock and shout, *Hey, everybody! This guy is a perbert!*"

"What's a perbert?" Caterina asked.

I thought about correcting them, but then they'd just google it when they got home, and I didn't want that. It seemed everyone had the idea, or hadn't made the leap to *pervert*, because no one said anything.

"I don't know," Betty said. "But they're really bad. And deserve to be hit in the head with a rock."

Judy stifled a grin. "But there are no rocks in here. What will you do then?"

Betty reached behind herself and pulled out a nasty-looking rock with sharp edges. "I usually have one on me."

"Where did you have that?" Kelly asked. To my surprise, she didn't confiscate it like she did all of Betty's other weapons. Maybe she felt better knowing the girl had it.

The other three girls also pulled rocks from behind them.

"We sewed pockets in our bows," Lauren said. "Just in case we came across any perberts."

"Or orangutans," Ava added. "Did you know you can't get insurance against orangutan attacks?"

Judy stared at the little girl. She must've known that was correct, considering she worked in insurance. I explained Ava's obsession with insurance, and the two began talking.

"You really should have orangutan insurance, though," Ava said.

"And insurance against perberts," Betty added.

Judy smiled. "I'll see what I can do."

The table broke into smaller conversations.

I got up and stretched and headed toward the stage. My goal was the yearbooks on a table there. Maybe I could find pictures of Brandon or Jason. It's too bad our name tags didn't have last names on them.

With one hundred or so classmates, it would take a while to go through, looking at first names only. And there were four books, one from each year, on the table. The display itself was a bit lame since the yearbooks and a couple of purple and gold crepe paper streamers were basically it. Someone had decided to go minimalist. Well, I nailed my job by recruiting my troop to check people in. I guess whoever set this up just didn't have the same standards I had.

Betty and Caterina appeared.

"What are you doing?" Betty asked.

I motioned for them to come closer. "There are four yearbooks to go through to see if Brandon and Jason are in them."

Caterina nodded. "We can do that."

Now why hadn't I thought of that? Brandon and Jason might be suspicious if I was poring through the yearbooks. But the kids were no threat. And they could claim curiosity.

I handed them the books, two each. "Good idea. Can you make it look like you're curious about Kelly and me?"

Caterina nodded. "We're good at pretending."

"Here." Betty handed me two wallets.

"What's this?" I turned toward the wall to look at them, and the girls stepped in front of me, their eyes on my classmates.

Betty looked at me as if I was an idiot. "They're Jason's and Brandon's."

"How did you get these?" I held one in each hand. They seemed light.

"Betty's been practicing pickpocketing," Caterina said. "Do you think there's a merit badge for that?"

"It's doubtful." And too bad. I could see this being a useful skill. "You mean you just walked up and slipped these out of their back pockets without them noticing?"

Betty looked at me curiously. "It's not like it's hard."

I could lift a wallet with some competence, but the idea that an eleven-year-old could pull it off put me to shame. I hadn't seen a move that smooth since Paula Pickpocket in the CIA. Pickpocket wasn't her name—it was more of a nickname (her real name was Kostantinopolus). Anyway, Paula could pick anything without being caught. She once lifted socks off of four really old men...at a nudist colony. They had no idea. And they were wearing shoes. To this day, people are torn between trying to figure it out and not wanting to know, ever.

"Keep an eye on Brandon and Jason for me."

"We've been doing that for a few minutes now," Betty said, as the two girls closed in.

Brandon's wallet was plain, black leather, and just had money in it. There wasn't a single credit card or ID. Not even a photo. Who just carries around cash? A spy, that's who. Often times, we even clipped the labels out of our clothes so that if we were found dead, no one would be able to guess the country of origin.

I handed that one back to Betty, who stuck it into the sash of her dress, next to the chalk pikes. Then I turned my attention to Jason's. This wallet was blue nylon, had thirty dollars all in one-dollar bills, an Illinois driver's license that read Jason Hess, and a military ID. I scrutinized it. The military ID had the name Jason Grosz. Now, why would he have two forms of government ID with two different names?

Was Jason a spy? A killer? Or both? And who in the hell was Brandon?

CHAPTER ELEVEN

The three of us walked back to the main table, and I watched as Betty managed to get the wallet into Jason's back pocket without him noticing. She was very slick. I don't think he felt a thing. Brandon, however, was very alert and watching everything, so she dropped his on the floor beneath his chair.

"Hey, dude." Betty tapped him on the shoulder, causing him to jump. "Your wallet's on the floor."

Brandon looked down and swept it up. "Thanks, kid. It must've fallen out of my pocket."

Did I just imagine it, or did Jason just reach back and touch his back pocket? Interesting.

"We've got Mrs. Wrath's and Mrs. Albers' yearbooks!" Caterina held them up.

Lauren and Ava dropped everything and crowded around her. I stared at Jason and Brandon, but they were both staring at me. I put on an exasperated face to play the part of the harassed, exhausted Girl Scout leader. It wasn't hard. I really was a harassed and exhausted leader.

"Cool!" Lauren said. "Now we can see what things were like in the olden days!"

Everyone at the table laughed, which broke the tension a bit. Even Ashley smiled. She walked over to the girls.

"You won't find her in there under Wrath. Her name was Czrygy. See?" Ashley opened the book to the right page and showed the girls a picture of me.

Oh, crap. I never took a good picture in school. Especially freshman year.

"This is our freshman year," Ashley continued with a giggle.

All four girls turned to stare at me as if I'd suddenly turned into a vampire.

"I can explain," I said.

Kelly started laughing. "That was your worst picture. You had braces, it was your first attempt at makeup, and your hair was…"

"Were you electrocuted?" Lauren asked as she held up the book for all to see.

I've been cursed with curly hair. No matter what I did, it didn't behave. Add humidity to that, which we'd had that August when the photo was taken, and you have a frizzy cloud that sort of orbits my head. No comment on the makeup. That was just a bad idea. The braces I couldn't help.

"You look like a mad scientist," Betty said. "Were you a mad scientist? Because that would be cool."

"Yes!" Lucinda chimed in. "Did she tell you how she burned off all my hair in chemistry?" She then went on to explain it to them.

"You were kind of a badass," Betty said. "Not like me, but kind of."

That was true. I'd never be as badass as Betty.

"Let's see the one from senior year." Ashley took the book from Caterina and brought it back to the table.

The girls gave me a look before whispering among themselves. I can only imagine that Betty was explaining what they had to do with the three other books.

"Look at Marla." Ashley pointed her out as she showed us the homecoming court. Her sister was next to Marla, with Ashley next to her. "She was such a bitch." She froze and looked at us apologetically.

"She totally was." Cindy patted her on the arm. "I don't think anyone liked her."

"And Marla didn't care what we thought," Judy added.

"She never distracted me from how I felt about Merry," Mitch added.

The whole table turned to look at him, then me. Maybe some of them hadn't heard his protestations of love yet and were just as surprised as I'd been.

We were going to have to have a serious talk about this.

"Poor Barry." Ashley pointed at a picture of him and Eddy grinning on the football field. "Who'd want to kill him?"

We all turned to look at his covered body on the floor. I'm not sure what we were hoping to see, but I know I'd have liked a neon sign that told us who'd killed him. That would've been helpful.

"And look at Eddy and Heather!" Lucinda said, drawing our attention back to the book. "He's going to be so upset when he comes to and finds out about Barry. They were best friends."

Judy studied the photo. "Why didn't Heather come?"

Lucinda and Ashley exchanged looks.

"What?" Judy pressed.

"She and Barry split up." Ashley leaned forward. "He'd been cheating on her for years. So she finally ran off to India and joined a commune."

Lucinda nodded. "And she married some swami or something."

"Really?" Cindy looked stunned.

"Well, that's what I'd heard." Lucinda shrugged.

I kind of remembered Heather. She had been one of the cheerleaders and friends with the twins and Lucinda.

Looking at Barry, only a few feet away from his friends, worried me. Especially seeing Eddy there. What was he going to think when he woke up to find his best friend dead? As far as he remembered, they were chatting with people they hadn't seen in years, then hallucinating before passing out. The last thing he would ever imagine would be waking up, to find out his best friend had been murdered. And that he hadn't been cognizant enough to help his best friend by fighting off the attacker.

Looking over at Kelly, it felt like the air had been sucked out of my lungs. I don't know what I'd do if I woke up to find her murdered body next to me. It would be devastating. It would haunt me for the rest of my life.

Ashley must be going through something similar, I realized with a start. In her case, her sister had been standing next to her. She sat down and breathed her last. And Ashley didn't even get a chance to say goodbye.

"What do you think Marla was going to say?" Cindy's voice snapped me out of my reverie and brought me back to the present as she handed Kevin another cupcake. "You know, the secrets thing?"

Mitch rolled his eyes. "She resented pretty much everyone in the class. It's no secret that no one liked her. But you might be surprised to learn she didn't like any of us either."

"Except for you," Lucinda said.

Mitch nodded. "I know it looked like that. She threw herself at me for four years. I don't think she liked me. I think she just saw me as some sort of trophy."

Dylan smirked. "Mitch Aiken, trophy boyfriend. I remember you famously turning her down in front of everyone at homecoming."

Cindy shot him a look. "He had good reason to because he was dating Lucinda."

Lucinda turned bright red and stared at me, mouthing the word *Sorry*. What the hell was that for?

"I'm sorry, Lucinda." Mitch rubbed my back. "I was just using you to make Merry jealous."

"Will you please stop?" I hissed and removed his hand from my person and got to my feet. "Can I speak with you for a moment, please?" I was getting tired of discussing this in front of an audience. Changing tactics and dealing with him one-on-one might work better.

"Uh-oh." Jason winked. "Girl trouble."

Mitch smiled and followed me to the other side of the gym.

"What is going on?" I demanded. "You and I were *never* a thing, and we won't *ever* be a thing. Why are you telling everyone something that isn't remotely true?"

Mitch studied me for a moment before answering. "I can't ignore my feelings, Merry. Or the past."

"Did you hit your head or something?" I asked, wondering if I should hit his head on something. "Because if you cared about me sometime in the past eleven years, you would've contacted me, which you didn't."

Mitch looked down at his feet. "I was too shy."

"You've got to be kidding me. You were never shy in high school. Hell, you weren't even shy just now when you bragged about Marla hanging on you."

Was Betty right in thinking that Mitch killed Marla and was shadowing me in an attempt to throw everyone off? I looked over at the table where Betty was arm wrestling…and winning, against Brandon.

"I don't know why you don't believe me." Mitch picked up my hand. "I'm totally sincere."

I resisted the urge to throw him across the room. Instead, I jerked my hand away.

"This is all I need. Three bodies, no cell service, locked in a gym with a guy who is pretending to pine for me. What else could go wrong?"

Mitch thought about this for a moment. "At least the lights haven't gone out."

There was a snap, and then it went pitch dark. And my knee "accidentally" connected with his groin. I heard an oof and a thud as he fell to the floor. It wasn't just because Mitch was driving me nuts—it was also a shrewd move to drop him if he was the killer. At least, that's what I was telling myself.

It was totally petty and immature, but since Kelly didn't see it, she couldn't call me those things. Meanwhile, the killer had plunged us into total darkness, and I only had one concern. Well, five.

I reached for my cell to turn on the flashlight but realized I'd left it on the table. Why weren't people pulling theirs out to light things up?

"Girls! Kelly!" I shouted. "Stick together, and hold hands! I'm coming for you."

I don't know if you've ever been in a gym at night when the lights go out. It's completely disorienting. Holding my hands in front of me, I raced across the floor until I collided with a table.

Of course, I took about four steps before I tripped over something and fell to the floor. Feeling around in the dark, I realized I'd tripped over one of my unconscious classmates. It was a big person because their bulk had cushioned my fall. I felt for a pulse to make sure they were alive and then got to my feet. They were going to have bruises in weird places later.

It took ten steps this time before I tripped and almost fell over another body. This was ridiculous. I thought about the gym layout to guess where I was. I'd dragged Mitch off to talk. We hadn't walked over any bodies, but we had been next to where Barry's corpse was. Instead of hugging the wall to get back to the table, I'd tripped over what I was guessing was Eddy Butz. Those two were outliers, on the edge of the group. I backtracked carefully, found Eddy, and got out of that whole mess.

Somebody finally turned on the flashlight on their cell, but it immediately went out.

"My battery's dead," I heard Cindy say. The others said the same thing. Why were their batteries dead? Had they been messing with their phones the whole time?

There were some sounds of panic coming from the others, but I didn't really care about them as long as my best friend and troop were safe.

"Right here, Mrs. Wrath!" Caterina's voice said as a tiny hand took hold of mine.

"All of us," Ava's voice said as another child took my other hand.

"Betty? Lauren?"

They both answered. Kelly, however, did not.

"Kelly?" I called out, but there was no answer. Damn. "Roll call! Answer when I call your name!"

There was a murmur of agreement. I called each and every name, and they all answered. Except for one. Kelly.

"Does anyone have a lighter or matches?" I asked as the *Exit* lights over the doors flickered on.

My eyes adjusted to see the very dim shapes of four little girls in front of me. A flash of light appeared on my left as a match sputtered to life, illuminating Dylan's face. He looked terrified.

I reached the table just as the lights turned back on. Everyone let out a sigh of relief for being able to see again. That's when I saw her. Kelly was facedown on the table with what looked like blood staining the back of her head.

She had a pulse, and her breathing was okay. She'd been stunned. Someone had hit my best friend.

And I was going to kill them.

CHAPTER TWELVE

There was a groan, and Kelly sat up slowly. "What happened?" She felt the back of her head and then looked at the blood on her hand. "Who hit me?"

Everyone was now crowded around the table, staring at her. Cindy was in Kevin's arms. Kevin was eyeing the last two cupcakes. Lucinda, Judy, and Ashley were clinging to the table. Mitch limped over to the table and sat down.

"Are you okay?" I stared into her eyes. "How many fingers am I holding up?"

"You aren't holding up any fingers," Kelly said irritably as she snatched some napkins and held them to the back of her head.

"The lights went out!" Cindy cried out.

"I remember that," Kelly said. "Then I felt pain and now this."

I glared at everyone around the table. One of these bastards hit my best friend. They'd tried to kill her!

Wait, they *tried*. They didn't succeed. Thank God for that. Why didn't they succeed? Maybe this was a way to distract me. The lights made that possible. But how did they turn them off? We were all at the table. It didn't make sense. Did they have some sort of remote?

What did make sense was the idea of distraction. Turning the lights out made us stop looking at the yearbooks. Did Jason or Brandon do that? Did one of them make an attempt on Kelly's life?

"Where are the light switches?" I asked as I looked around the gym.

"I'll show you." Mitch took my hand and led me away.

I dropped his hand but continued following as he led me over to a nasty-looking series of at least a dozen switches between the bleachers and second set of doors to the lobby.

"We would've seen someone if they came over here." I studied the panel. "I don't remember anyone leaving the table before the lights went out."

Mitch leaned in. His construction background had come in handy for the explanation of why the phones didn't work. Maybe he'd know how this happened.

"See this wire?" He pointed to a tiny little antenna-looking wire coming out from behind the panel. "Someone rigged it to work the lights wirelessly."

I straightened up. "Like a remote." I looked back at the table, and an idea occurred to me. I just didn't want to share this with Mitch. He could be the killer, but I knew that he hadn't made it to the table before I had. Not in the condition I'd left him in.

"Let's head back to the others," I said, turning away before he could make a play for my hand or anything else.

"Just like old times, eh?" Mitch winked as he caught up to me.

I stopped. "This really has to stop." Mostly because I was getting a little jealous. If I'd dated Mitch, I wanted to access those memories. But I hadn't, and it was making me mad that he had some memories of something that never happened.

Mitch held up his hands defensively. "Okay. I'll stop."

It was that easy?

"Exactly what fictional memories do you have of us dating?" I had to admit I was curious. Maybe I could live vicariously through his delusion.

He smiled. "We liked to go to Oleo's a couple of nights a week for romantic dinners. You helped me study for English class. And then there were those nights where we'd go make out at some abandoned cornfield." He wiggled his eyebrows suggestively.

It kind of sucked that I couldn't enjoy "remembering" these things too. Mitch was gorgeous. He was one of the few guys in our class who'd kept his shape…and his hair. But I really wasn't interested. Rex was ten times the man this guy was.

I felt a twinge of guilt, but shook it off. I had nothing to feel bad for.

"Are you on some new kind of medication?" I asked. "Were you ever in a coma? Did you drink the punch? Were you kidnapped by aliens?"

Mitch laughed. "Nope. Perfectly healthy and sane."

Great. I headed back to the others.

Kelly stood up and drew me aside. "Did you see anything?"

"Yeah. Mitch said the panel might be configured to operate remotely."

Kelly saw where this was going. "Someone has a remote on them."

I nodded. "And the keys. I can't believe I didn't think of that before. We need to search people."

"I'm on it." Betty, who'd appeared out of nowhere, clapped her hands and rubbed them together. "Strip search time."

"Uh, no. You aren't strip searching anyone."

She ignored me. "Starting with that Mitch guy."

I grabbed her by the arm and pulled her back. "I've got a better idea. Get the other girls and Kevin together."

As she skipped away, I told Kelly, "We need to start taking pictures. I should've thought of that sooner. But it's a good job to keep Betty from thoroughly searching the adults."

"Normally," Kelly said as she rubbed the back of her head, "I'd disagree with involving the girls further. But you might be right. Besides, if we all end up murdered, that will leave a record behind."

"Do you really think we'll all be murdered?" I wondered. "I don't think it will get that far. But you are to stick close to me until we find that remote." I thought for a moment. "Something's bothering me. Why didn't anyone turn on the flashlights from their phones? I know a couple said their phones were dead."

Kelly winced as she touched the back of her head. "Maybe we were all so used to them not working, we didn't think about it."

That seemed plausible, maybe. "Man. We really are screwing this up in so many ways. We should've searched for the keys way back when this first started."

Kelly looked grim. "There's been so much happening that we haven't had time to think. The killer is constantly distracting us so that we won't puzzle this out."

She might be right. "Do you think there was an attempt on your life?" I asked. "Were you the next victim?"

She shook her head and then winced from the pain. "For some reason, I don't think so. Weird, huh?"

Betty, Lauren, Caterina, and Ava appeared, dragging Kevin behind them.

"What's the plan?" Ava asked.

I got down on their level. "I need you guys to stick together and, starting with Marla's body, take lots of photos of the crime scenes and the gym as a whole." I pointed toward the lights panel. "Make sure you get that too."

Betty took my cell and nodded. "We started taking pictures with your phone earlier in the night."

I frowned. "No, I've had my phone with me this whole time."

Betty didn't miss a beat. "Of course you did."

Great. The girls probably took a million very unflattering photos of me. I'd need to delete them before they showed up…anywhere.

"Right," Kevin said. "I'll secure the food."

"No, we won't be in here too much longer, even if I have to chip away at the walls with a spork," I said. "You are supervising."

All four girls froze and stared at me. They must've been shocked that I was putting Kevin Dooley in charge. That's when I noticed that Kevin was looking at me the same way.

"I want an adult with them for safety," I explained.

Kevin looked around. "Mitch would be good. He's big. Looks like James Bond."

"You." I pointed at him. "Are the adult. And a police officer."

The realization slowly dawned on him like an *a-ha* moment, and he nodded.

Betty rolled her eyes and took my cell. "Whatever. Come on, Officer Dooley."

"Okay," he said as he loped along behind them.

Kelly watched as they scampered toward the stage. "What are we going to do?"

"We," I said as I fixed my eyes on the group surrounding the table, "are about to make some grown adults very angry."

CHAPTER THIRTEEN

I looked around the table. Cindy, Judy, Mitch, Lucinda, Veronica, Ashley, Brandon, Jason, and Dylan all looked back. This was my suspect pool. Kelly, the girls, and even Kevin Dooley were eliminated. Oh sure, I wouldn't put it past Betty to pull this off if she were murdery, but if she had, not only would all of us be dead, but the crime would be unsolvable.

Of the nine suspects, Brandon and Jason were still on the top of my list, but to be fair, I really hadn't seen any of these people, with the exception of my real estate agent, Veronica, in eleven years. What did I really know about any of them, except for the fact that one of them was behind all of this.

"What do we do now?" Judy asked me.

She and Cindy had been casting nervous glances at Jason and Brandon. I couldn't blame them. Especially now that Kelly had been hit.

"I propose a little test of faith," I suggested. "Everyone needs to turn out their pockets and purses. Someone here has the keys to this building and a remote for the lights." I pointed downward at the table. "This ends here. Now."

Kelly didn't wait. She upended her purse onto the table. It was tiny and just held some credit cards, cash, her phone, and some tissues. Since most of the women also brought small evening purses, this shouldn't take too long.

I dumped my small bag on the table. There were my car keys, a bottle of aspirin (because I hadn't been that optimistic as to how this night would go—and boy, was I right), a Twinkie, some cash, and a Swiss Army knife.

"You have a knife!" Ashley scooted backward.

"You have a Dora the Explorer keychain?" Jason asked.

"No one has been killed with a knife," Cindy chastised gently. "I have one of those too." And she dumped out her purse, which revealed a makeup kit, hairspray, a bottle of Evian facial spritz water, a bottle of very expensive perfume, a wallet, a hotel key, car keys, and a tin of mints.

Jason was still shaking his head, looking amused. "Dora the Explorer?" He snorted.

"I like Dora!" I grumbled.

And I did. Dora was kind of my spirit animal. I'd always suspected that she was a spy, the way she moved around the world, and that Boots, the monkey, was her handler. I had Dora pajamas, and when I'd first moved back home, my first house had Dora the Explorer bedsheets as living room curtains. Kelly'd made me take them down.

Lucinda didn't say anything. She dumped her purse on the table, and it had all the same things as ours, with more makeup. "I didn't drive, so I don't have keys." She pointed at one of the women still passed out on the floor. "She's my ride."

"I'm not doing this!" Ashley shook her head vigorously. "It's against my rights!"

"Oh, hell!" Judy turned her purse upside down. There were five packs of unfiltered cigarettes, gum, money, and a corkscrew. "Let's just get this over with."

Ashley shook her head again. "This isn't right. You can't make us."

Cindy glared at her. "We happen to have law enforcement here who could make you."

I looked across the room where I spotted Kevin, who looked like he was asleep standing up. He sniffed the air, and his eyes shot open. He'd seen something. I braced myself. Maybe he'd found a weapon or spotted a remote?

Kevin moved forward, his eyes locked on something on the other side of one of the tables. The tablecloth made it impossible to see what the target was. Could this be the moment Kevin earns his job title? He got down on the floor and crawled behind the table. Two seconds later he jumped to his feet, holding something in his hand high over his head.

"Found it!" he shouted.

"What is it?" I wanted to run over and look, but I needed to focus on getting these people to turn out their pockets.

"A peanut!" He smiled before popping it into his mouth.

I turned back to the table and looked at Mitch.

He shrugged and emptied his pockets. All he had were car keys and a wallet. "Do you want to search me, Merry?" He winked.

Sure. If I could do it while slapping him. Slap-frisking, believe it or not, is a real thing in a remote area of Chechnya. Just before you pat a person down, you slap them. You repeat this after frisking their arms, torso, hips, and legs. I've never really gotten a clear answer on why they do this, but it has something to do with goats—like everything else in Chechnya.

Jason and Brandon also shook their heads. Dylan looked like he was torn.

"Guys," I said with exasperation. "If you don't do it, you look guilty, plain and simple."

Dylan said, "I don't know. It's so authoritarian."

"How do we know *you* haven't hidden the remote thingy or the keys somewhere before you asked us to do this?" Ashley snapped.

Judy rolled her eyes. "If you aren't guilty, just open your purse."

Ashley burst into tears. "Amanda would back me up! She wouldn't let you make me!"

That was a very effective way to get us to back off because it seemed cruel to imply any guilt with her twin dead in the same room.

Dylan, sensing that he still had a chance with her, put his arm around her. "Stop picking on Ashley! If she isn't doing it, I won't either."

Jason and Brandon nodded in agreement.

Mitch stood up and looked menacing. "If Merry wants you to do it, you need to do it." He motioned to the rest of us. "We all did it. What are you hiding?"

Well, this was new. Mitch had been playing the affable, handsome/concerned imaginary ex-boyfriend this whole time. With his height and physique, he really did come across as a force to be reckoned with. Were there other sides he'd been holding back? Like the one that has an inclination to murder people he hadn't seen in eleven years?

Brandon and Jason stood up and glared back. I guess they thought they could handle him together, even though their eyes had a hint of doubt.

"I said, no!" Jason clenched his fist. "What's next? You going through our wallets?"

Already done. But with his fury at its peak, it didn't seem like a good time to tell him that. I gave silent thanks to the criminal side of Betty.

"We have three dead people." Kelly narrowed her eyes. "And I was next. We don't have time for pleasantries!"

I pointed at her and nodded my head. It was a good point. She was the only victim who'd survived an attack. Ashley burst into a fresh batch of tears and buried her head against Dylan's shoulder. Dylan had a blissed-out look on his face. He probably never dreamed he'd come to the reunion and end up dating a grieving cheerleader.

"Want me to make them do it, Merry?" Mitch, who was still in a face-off with Brandon and Jason, growled.

"Forget it," I said, motioning for everyone to sit. "At least we now know five people who are innocent." I nodded toward Barry's body, where Kevin watched the girls take pictures. "And those five too."

"That's not right!" Jason pounded on the table. "You can't accuse the four of us without proof!"

"Yeah!" Brandon echoed.

Personally, if I'd wanted to push it, these clowns would all be lined up against the gym wall and frisked while Betty shoved sharpened chalk sticks into sensitive, soft places. Searching someone is trickier than you think. In the world of international espionage, a simple pat down frisk wouldn't cut it. You had to be *thorough*.

Bad guys rarely stuffed contraband in their pockets because it was so obvious. I once knew a Turkish terrorist who kept a razor blade hidden in a Rolex wristwatch, a Bolivian double agent who hid flash drives in her elaborately styled bouffant, and a Chechen who hid an Uzi in a place you'd never ever want to search.

But I wasn't sure that manhandling my classmates was worth it. Forcing Ashley, who'd just lost her sister, to do anything would come off as unsympathetic and mean because she wasn't in her right mind. I could understand why. I'd be devastated if whoever had hit Kelly had killed her. My stomach sank at the thought. I could never lose my best friend. That's it. I made a mental note to die first.

The girls returned and handed me my phone. If they wondered why we were all glaring at each other, they didn't say. Kevin plopped down next to Cindy, leaned his head back, and fell asleep.

Betty and the others collected up the yearbooks and sat on the floor as they quietly leafed through them. At least that would provide some solid evidence. But of what? What if Jason and Brandon were crashing? Did that make them killers?

Perhaps one of them knew a classmate or two and had decided to crash. It was possible, I guess, that they could be lookie-loos. And if so, did they know each other before coming here? How could I find out? If the girls proved that one of them wasn't in the yearbooks, then what?

And their wallets…what were the odds that they were both unusual? Brandon's being devoid of anything but cash, and Jason had a military ID with a totally different last name. I'd known a number of military personnel from my stint in the CIA. They'd talked about how rigid the system was. It was practically impossible to fake a military ID, one of them had told me. It was easier to forge a driver's license.

Now I really wanted to see that license again. From what I remembered it had seemed legit, complete with multiple holograms—which are near impossible to forge. Which was the real Jason? Jason Hess or Jason Grosz? Before this was over, I was going to have a little chat with Jason.

The real problem was Ashley's refusal. I totally understood it, as she was completely distraught and not in her right mind. People who experience a sudden, tragic loss can become inflexible in an attempt to regain some control in a situation they have no control over. But it gave the others a reason to also refuse to be searched. That was a problem.

What would Rex do? He'd probably have the wherewithal to search them, either by talking them into it or arresting them and confiscating their belongings. I really wished he were here. I wasn't sure what the law said about things like trying to search classmates you knew eleven years ago while at a reunion where you were locked in with dead people.

I could wake up Kevin and have him arrest the four who refused, but on what grounds? That I didn't remember two of them? That they refused to offer up their belongings? I was pretty sure that wouldn't hold up in court. And it could lead to a possible lawsuit against me.

I'd always had law enforcement to back me up when I needed it. Oh sure, they didn't like me galivanting around, getting in trouble. But in this case, I was completely on my own. And for once, I didn't like it.

Kelly got to her feet and began picking up the punch cups that littered the floor.

"What are you doing?" I asked.

"You've got pictures for law enforcement," she said with a sigh. "I need something to do."

"I'll help!" Cindy got up and joined her. The two of them began picking up the cups that had been dropped by our immobilized classmates. As they went, I noticed Kelly taking pulses. I didn't blame her, but crossed my fingers behind my back in hoping she wouldn't find another person dead.

"I'll help too." Judy got up and grabbed the nearest trash can and dragged it over. As it bumped along, an idea hit me.

"Hold it!" I ran over and dove headfirst into the can. When I came up, I held a tiny remote control in my hand. It was soaking wet from being dropped into a cup of punch. My guess was that it wouldn't function again.

"Is that it?" Kelly asked.

Mitch joined me. I wrapped it in a napkin and showed it to him.

"Something like that would work." He nodded.

I looked around to make a mental picture of where everyone was and depressed the large button in the middle.

We were plunged into darkness. I immediately turned the lights back on. Nothing had changed, and I let out a breath. I couldn't believe it would work soaking wet.

Judy looked at the can. "It was right next to the table. Anyone could've thrown it in there."

She wasn't wrong. I tried to recall if I'd heard something like that dropped into the can. But with the shock of complete darkness, my tripping over bodies, and fear for the girls and Kelly, I hadn't thought of anything else.

"Well, we know now that it's one of us," I said. "We still haven't found the keys though." I glared at the four who'd rejected the search.

All four of them had the good grace to look away. Lucky for them I was too conflicted to force them into a possible illegal situation. What was unlucky for all of us was that, even now, we were no closer to finding the killer.

And that totally sucked.

CHAPTER FOURTEEN

I needed to do something. Well, something other than cleaning up. We had three bodies and a few dozen unconscious classmates on the floor. And we had four people blocking the investigation.

All I had was a remote, three bodies, and two weapons. What I didn't have was a motive. I still thought it had something to do with Marla's speech. It felt like that was important. One of my theories was that all this had been done to shut Marla up before she exposed a secret that was worth killing her for.

What were those secrets? I had found Marla's in her purse. Firing because of embezzlement would've probably ended her career for life. Is that what someone with a big secret does? Out other people's secrets?

My only secret wasn't really a secret anymore—that was my involvement in the CIA. Kelly didn't have any deep dark secrets, or I would know. The idea of blackmailing the girls was ridiculous since no one but me knew they were coming. As for Kevin? He displays all of his bad behavior unashamedly. There'd be nothing else to tell unless he was moonlighting as a double agent or porn star. I threw up in my mouth a little at that last idea.

I thought about the others. What were they hiding? And was it enough to knock off Marla? Just Marla. It seemed like Barry, Amanda, and Kelly had little to do with her.

Which brought back the idea of a spree killer. I didn't know much about them, and I didn't want to ask Betty just yet. But from what I understood, a spree killer kills as many people as possible in a short period of time. Which would mean that Marla's secrets had nothing to do with her murder.

Then again, maybe after killing Marla to shut her up, the killer kind of liked it and decided to knock off the others.

That's all I had—killing to keep Marla quiet and spree killer. It sounded crazy. On the plus side, it was only two motives that could even be blended, which seemed like a bit of a win.

Okay, if Marla had blackmail material on so many of my classmates, she'd have to have notes, right? As a former spy, I'd trained myself to memorize a lot, from a complete cover story, a new address and name every few weeks, or where to avoid the Komodo dragon when navigating the Yakuza boss's secret hideaway.

But the idea that Marla was able to memorize a list of grievances and juicy material was a bit far-fetched. Like most people, she had to have a written speech. I hadn't found anything like that in her purse. If I were Marla, I would've hidden it someplace not so obvious.

Which left two places—the dressing room beneath the stage and the locker room. I thought about this. I didn't remember Marla being a jock in school. But she did have a tendency for the theatrical and her purse was there, so I needed to get down to the green room for another once-over.

"Hey, Merry..." Kelly called out.

I gave her the thumbs-up. "You're doing great!"

Since I couldn't just sit here and watch the three women clean up without feeling a tiny bit guilty, I got to my feet and walked over.

"At last." Kelly motioned to the rest of the gym. "Can you clear off the tables? I..."

"Oh!" I looked back at where I'd been sitting. "You wanted me to clean up!"

With a sigh, she said, "What did you think I was going to say?"

I shrugged. "I don't know. Hey, Merry, can you hurry this investigation up? Merry, do you have any aspirin? Merry, can you make sure Betty doesn't inadvertently kill anyone with sharpened chalk?"

Kelly looked around me and, seeing the girls still sitting on the floor, reading the yearbooks, turned back to me. "Why are you over here, then?"

"I'm going to search the room under the stage to see if I can find Marla's speech."

Kelly wiped a stray strand of hair from her eyes. "Do you really think that's the motive?"

"You have a better idea?" I put my hands on my hips. "Other than Betty's spree killer theory?"

Her eyes once again found the girls. "Normally, something like that would worry me. But tonight? Not so much."

"She's advancing in the dark arts, that's for sure." I tugged on my dress. "This was the wrong thing to wear."

"At least yours goes to your knees," Kelly pointed out. "Mine's too short. It keeps riding up."

"Maybe I can find some gym clothes in the locker room?" I wondered.

Kelly made a face. "And wear something a teenager hasn't taken home to wash all semester? No thanks. I'd rather trade clothes with Barry."

I scanned the floor. "Why don't you trade with one of those girls wearing jeans?"

Her jaw dropped open. "Strip one of the passed out people?"

"Well, yeah. Tell them you switched clothes in an LSD-enhanced state."

You had to get clothes where you could. I can't tell you how many times I'd had to run out of a sauna in Sweden, wearing nothing but a towel…in February, with nary a clothesline full of convenient clothing in sight.

On several occasions, Riley, my former handler, was run out of a house buck naked. Most of those situations were because the husband of the wife he was pumping for intel had come home, and Riley had lost track of time. In Buenos Aires, he had to walk nude, through the city streets, before he found a lime green muumuu hanging on a line. When he walked into the office, I took some pictures that are still in a safety deposit box in Switzerland. Someday, I might even use them.

"I don't think so," Kelly said. "I'll just stay in this uncomfortable dress until you figure out how to get us out of here. Hurry up, please."

"I'm going to check out the dressing room to see if I can find Marla's speech. Keep an eye on everyone, and let me know if someone comes after me."

"How am I supposed to do that?" Kelly asked.

"I have no idea," I replied. "But I'm sure you'll think of something."

Hopefully, the killer would be seen sneaking off toward the stage, and then we'd have him. It's not that I was being cavalier in hoping that whoever killed my classmates would attempt to murder me as well, but I knew I could handle myself. If not, I could scream like the dickens, and someone would come running.

I passed by Marla's body toward the back of the stage, where I found the trap door and heaved it open. In a matter of moments, I was standing at the bottom of the stairs, looking around the room.

It hadn't changed since I'd seen it last. But then again, I'd only been down here for five minutes earlier. Marla's purse wasn't there anymore, but we knew the speech wasn't in it. She must have hidden it somewhere.

Everyone was still in the gym, but a thought jolted me. What if the killer wasn't part of that group? What if it was an outsider? Could someone be hiding from us, coming out only to kill or strike?

That would suck. Okay, so it wouldn't because it would mean my classmates weren't guilty. But it would because my suspect list would be useless. I gave this new theory some thought. Sure, the killer has been outside the gym, but in here where could a stranger actually hide? The lockers in the locker room weren't big enough to hold anyone larger than my troop. It was the only place besides this dressing room that would provide cover.

This theory wasn't my greatest idea. Actually, my greatest idea was bugging MI6 in London, utilizing tea bags for mics. The English love their tea and never suspected a thing, and it proved to be a very useful way to keep tabs on one of our allies. We did lose a couple of bugs to hot water. Fortunately, because we used actual tea, no one was the wiser.

The reason the theory of the hidden stranger wouldn't work was due to the fact that there were so few of us—every single person would notice a stranger. But, just in case, I needed to clear the dressing room to make sure.

I searched all the areas that were big enough to hide a person, from behind the makeup tables to the racks of costumes. I was just going through the last rack when...

"What are we doing?" Betty asked behind me.

I must've jumped five feet in the air. Betty didn't so much as blink in reaction.

"What are you doing here?" I said once I regained my senses.

"I saw you go off alone, so I decided to go after you to protect you."

My curiosity was piqued. "How would you protect me?"

She looked around. "I'd rig up booby traps." She smiled and giggled. "Booby." Betty giggled again.

It seemed a tad unprofessional.

"You'd need time in advance to rig...um...traps. Which means you'd have to know that you'd need them." I eyed her carefully. "You didn't, did you? Know that this was all going to happen?" Of course I didn't think Betty had inside knowledge on the murders. She would've told me. At least, I think she would've.

The little girl shook her head. "No. I didn't know about this. But I do know how to set traps."

She wasn't wrong. I'd once been rendered unconscious by one of her traps that not only hit me hard, but also deployed a mist of chloroform. And that had been in her bedroom closet. It was always a good idea not to underestimate Betty.

I sat down at one of the makeup tables. "How would you physically protect me from a killer?" I wasn't being patronizing. I really was curious.

"I could shove them up against the wall with a chair," the kid said. "Like a lion tamer. Or I could use the sharp end of the makeup brushes to stab them in the throat." She took a very fluffy brush from a jar and demonstrated. She frowned at the dull end of the brush. "These need sharpening."

I took the brush from her and put it back. "Where do you come up with this stuff?" I wanted to add that it was too bad the CIA didn't have a junior spy program. But I didn't want to encourage the kid.

Betty shrugged. "I've been looking stuff up. Just to be ready. It's in our scout motto—be prepared."

"That usually applies to things like packing the right supplies for camping or making sure there's always a first aid kit wherever we go," I pointed out.

"Or it could apply to weapons." She pulled a set of brass knuckles out from her sash and fitted it over her fingers. "Like this."

"Where did you get those?" I examined her hand. "It's kid-sized! I never knew they made them that small."

"I found them somewhere," Betty said with a look that implied it was in my best interest not to know more.

I studied her. "They don't sell things like this on Amazon. That's a custom build. You didn't order these using my credit card, did you?"

She shook her head. "Not this time." Betty retrieved the weapon and stuffed it back into her sash. "What are we looking for?"

For a moment I thought about sending her back. I couldn't see Kelly giving her permission to join me. Then again, a fresh perspective might come in handy, even it if was an eleven-year-old's.

"I was thinking Marla might've had notes for her upcoming speech. It could be the killer's reason for taking her out."

The little girl nodded. "She had, like, dirt on everyone, right? She probably did have a speech or something. It's a good thing I'm here. You need me."

"Why do I need you?" It was a little insulting. "I was in the CIA for nearly ten years."

Betty folded her arms over her chest. "Yes, but when's the last time you were in a school?"

She had a point. "But Marla was my age. She hadn't been in a school either."

Betty snapped on a pair of latex gloves I didn't know she had. I should probably frisk her at some point, just in case she was also hiding cyanide, a dagger, or an AK-47. "Well, she'd known enough to hide her purse down here."

That was true.

"Besides." Betty looked thoughtful. "I probably know a lot more about mean girls than you do."

That was most likely also true. The girls had told me stories about Betty vanquishing mean girls on the playground. It was impressive how she did it without getting into trouble. According to the troop, Betty was a master at inventing "accidents" on the slide, monkey bars, and even the four-square court. And in each case, she'd managed to threaten the girl before a teacher arrived. Bullies rarely came close to my troop.

Betty looked me in the eye. "But before I find the speech, what's with you and that Mitch guy?"

I shook my head. "Nothing. We never dated in high school. In fact, I'm pretty sure he had no idea I existed back then. Now he's acting like we had this amazing love affair. I have no idea why he's lying, but if he doesn't stop, I may have to borrow your brass knuckles."

She tapped her chin thoughtfully. "In my experience, if a dude lies in public, they also lie in secret."

Lie in secret? "How would anyone know if you lied in secret?" I asked.

"Which means..." Betty ignored the question. "That he's a liar. We had this kid in our class...I'm not at liberty to say his name—but it was Oscar."

"Who's Oscar?"

Betty sighed as if I was annoying her. "He's a jerk. Anyway, Oscar lies all the time. And then my pudding went missing from my lunch. I knew it was Oscar. So I threatened to set his shoes on fire. And my pudding never went missing again."

"You threatened to set a kid's shoes on fire?" Why was I not surprised?

"While he was wearing them," Betty added.

That seemed extreme, even for Betty. "I'm not sure that's a good idea. Why when he's wearing them?"

Betty rolled her eyes. "Uh, because it was *butterscotch*. Do you know how hard that is to find? I only get it when Mom can find it, which is, like, once every couple of months. And I really, really like butterscotch."

Now I was craving butterscotch. It had been years since I'd had butterscotch pudding. The first thing I was going to do when this was over…if I wasn't dead…would be to find butterscotch-flavored anything.

Betty asked, "Mitch the hottie is hitting you with all these lies, right?"

He really was distracting me. Every time he flirted with me, it drove me nuts.

She took my silence for my answer. "And because he's bugging you, you're avoiding him. Which means you aren't studying him as a suspect."

Huh. "That's true. I have been avoiding him because he's so annoying. I've been looking at other people as suspects."

"You're welcome," Betty said as she climbed onto one of the chairs and reached up into the low ceiling rafters. "I won't charge you my usual fee this time. 'Cuz you're my leader and all."

"You charge people for your opinions?" My jaw dropped. "And they pay you?"

She was concentrating on feeling around the beams. "Of course. How else could I afford the brass knuckles?"

This brought me up short. "What's your going rate?"

Betty stuck her tongue out as she concentrated on her search. "A fee based on your age. Kids like me pay only a quarter. But I'd charge an adult like you twenty-five bucks."

I whistled. "Seems like I missed an opportunity when I was a kid." I'd usually traded information for things like free lemonade or the occasional puppy.

"Don't feel bad," Betty said. "You're pretty old. Like my grandma. You probably have alls hammers or demented stuff."

I folded my arms over my chest. My troop was convinced that Kelly and I were so old we were going to die soon. On more than one occasion they'd asked me to write them into my will since I didn't have any kids. But turning my spy equipment, which included things like a spatula flame thrower, over to ten-year-olds after my death seemed a tad irresponsible. Then again, I'd be dead, so maybe it didn't matter.

After feeling around for a moment, Betty pulled out a large envelope and handed it to me. Then she got down and looked at me expectantly. The envelope said:

Marla's Speech—Where Everyone Finally Gets Theirs

It couldn't get much more obvious than that. "How did you know that was up there?"

Betty shrugged. "I don't know. I just looked up and thought that's where I'd hide something." She thought for a moment. "Not something dumb like a speech though. Something useful—nunchucks."

I nodded because that made sense.

The trap door opened, and I shoved Betty behind me. I needn't have worried. Three pairs of tiny feet came down into the green room, followed by Kelly.

"What are you all doing here?" I asked. "You guys should've stayed out there."

Kelly rolled her eyes. "Oh yeah, like that's going to dissuade them."

That was true. "What about the others? Has anyone asked where I was? Where did you tell them you were going?"

"I told them we were going to look backstage to see if Marla hid more food here. People are getting hungry," Kelly said. "Besides, I wanted to keep the girls together. I don't know what to think about anyone out there."

"We're not in danger." Lauren shook her head. "The killer is just murdering old people!"

The other three nodded.

"Unless it's a spree killer," Betty added, and they agreed.

"Did you find anything in the yearbooks?" I asked.

Lauren shook her head. "There are two Brandons, both wearing glasses, both with red hair. He could be one of them."

"And five Jasons who all look as boring as this guy," Ava added. "Two of them were Jason Hess."

"Damn," I swore. "I really liked that idea."

"It doesn't mean it's them," Kelly said. "An imposter could've gotten hold of a yearbook. They have a whole section of them at the library."

I thought about this. "That's true. But the idea of those two as crashers is much harder to prove now that they're in the yearbook."

"I found something." Betty stepped forward and pointed at me. "Show her, Mrs. Wrath."

I was just showing Kelly the envelope when Kevin Dooley's head appeared upside down in the doorway.

"Any food down there?" he asked hopefully.

"Yes," I replied. "Food for thought."

Which was okay because I was pretty sure that whatever was in this speech would make everyone lose their appetites. It was time to see who had it in for Marla.

CHAPTER FIFTEEN

Back in the gym, we joined the group and sat at the table. I held up the envelope Betty had found.

"This was Marla's speech—the one where she was going to drop all kinds of secrets." I watched each and every face. Many of them had gone pale.

"I didn't read it," I assured them. "For the sake of transparency, I thought I'd read it aloud. But only if you agree. We don't have to read it at all."

Mitch shuddered. "Then I say we don't read it."

Judy elbowed him. "But this might give us a clue to who the killer is. I think Merry should read it."

Dylan raised his hand. "I vote for reading it."

"Oh sure." Cindy rolled her eyes. "Because you weren't mentioned in her tirade."

"Does that mean *you* don't want it read?" he asked her.

"I vote for Merry to read it," Cindy answered while glaring at Dylan.

Jason and Brandon nodded, but said nothing.

Ashley and Lucinda gave each other looks. At last Ashley said, "I vote that we read it."

Lucinda sighed. "I don't care either way."

Kelly and Kevin nodded at me, although I got the impression that Kevin thought he was agreeing to something else—like ordering pizza. He picked up a napkin with a few cupcake crumbs and started licking it.

"The ayes have it." I looked at the girls. "Do you think we should send them to the locker room or something?"

Kelly nodded. "Girls, can you go over to the stage and sit for a moment?"

"Hey!" Betty said. "I found it. I get to hear it."

Judy smiled at the girl. "I'm sorry, kiddo, but this is adult stuff."

Betty looked at her, then me. "So you're cutting us out of the action." She stamped her foot. "I'm not going anywhere."

I leaned over and whispered in her ear. "Should I tell Mrs. Albers about the brass knuckles?"

Betty narrowed her eyes. Kelly was always confiscating Betty's various weaponry. "Fine. But we'll be watching."

We waited for them to settle on the edge of the stage before I opened the envelope.

"I think if things get too juicy," Kelly said, "you should edit those parts out."

"Good idea," I agreed. "Betty could be listening."

Cindy looked at the stage. "From all the way over there?"

"You have no idea who we're dealing with." She probably had me bugged. At least, that's what I'd do if I were her.

Ashley held her hands out. "Before we begin, there's something we need to agree on. We need to promise that what's said here never leaves here. Okay?"

Everyone agreed. I slid a sheet of paper out of the envelope.

Judy breathed out. "At least it's only one sheet of paper."

I wanted to tell her she shouldn't get too comfortable with that. In the past, I've seen as little as five words topple regimes, get people killed and, in one case, staked outside to be tortured by goats. Okay, so it wasn't a very good torture because the goats basically tickled me with their beards and searched my clothes for food before munching on my shoes. The next day, when the surprised Uzbeks found me still alive (and shoeless), they released me, thinking it was the will of God. Kind of like Daniel in the lion's den…but much smellier.

I took a deep breath and began to read.

All of you think you're so smart! I know you never liked me. And why? Because I was such a good leader? You knew that or you wouldn't have voted for me. Or was it because I was the prettiest girl in the school?

This earned a snort from Lucinda and Ashley.

Whatever the reasons for your infantile jealousy, I want you to know that I was always better than you.

I paused. "This from a woman who'd just lost her job because she was embezzling."

"What?" Cindy asked.

I told them the whole story. Lucinda suggested I leak the notice from the brokerage firm to the press (aka her), but Kelly vetoed that idea. It did lighten the mood, however, so I continued to read.

And here's why:

I paused again. "I think I should just read about the people at this table." I glanced at our classmates passed out on the floor. "It isn't fair to read about them since they can't really defend themselves."

Lucinda and Ashley looked like they wanted to argue this point, so I waited. Kelly and Judy insisted that we keep the rest a secret until our classmates came to. I pointed out that, even then, I thought we should leave things alone. Those people were going to have miserable headaches and pain from lying on the hard gym floor for hours.

After a few tense moments, the women agreed, and I continued.

Lucinda slept her way to her anchor position at the TV station! The no-talent hack is just a slut who used three different men to work her way up from intern to anchor!

Lucinda laughed. "Is that all? That's old gossip. This isn't as bad as I thought."

A tremor of relief rippled around the table, and we all breathed a little easier. Of course Marla would say something like that. She was cruel and petty, and I hoped the rest of this was the same—just vicious rumors. Maybe Lucinda was right.

"If that isn't true," Jason figured, "then we have no reason to think the rest of the stuff she wrote is."

"Oh, I didn't say it wasn't true," Lucinda said without thinking. "I just said it's old gossip."

No one said anything for a few seconds. Well, if it didn't bother her, why should we let it bother us? I went on.

Mitch killed a man in Waterloo!

We all turned our attention on him. The color washed out of his face, and he held up his hands in protest. "Wait—hold on! That's not true!"

"Killing a guy is a lot worse than being a slut," Brandon reasoned.

"Thank you." Lucinda patted his arm.

"I didn't kill anyone!" Mitch began to sweat. "It wasn't like that at all. It was an accident on the construction site. He fell from a scaffold three stories up."

Jason leaned in. "Why did she think you did it? Were you there? If Lucinda's scandal is true, yours must be. Right?"

Mitch looked around the table, his eyes pleading for help, but there was none. Maybe Betty was right about him. He deflected suspicion by irritating me.

"Okay. Alright." Mitch rubbed his face with both hands. "I was on the scaffold too. But I was nowhere near him! An investigation cleared me of all wrongdoing!"

Dylan snorted. "Yeah, right. You probably paid off the police!"

"Why don't you believe me? Mine was an accident. What about what Lucinda did?" Mitch protested.

Ashley frowned. "What she did isn't a crime. You straight up murdered someone!"

Mitch slammed his fist on the table. "I didn't kill that guy! I wasn't anywhere near him. Lucinda's right. Marla just mined some old gossip."

I looked at Mitch for a long minute. Without the internet, none of us could check out his story.

"Let's keep going," I said.

Cindy married an old rich man, knocked him off, and had liposuction!

"Is that true?" Ashley looked more impressed than shocked. "How did you find an old rich guy? They never come to the mall."

Cindy spread her hands open. "I was never married, but I did date an older gentleman a long time ago. He had a heart attack while playing golf with some friends. I did have liposuction, so she's half right. Seriously, is she just making things up?"

Mitch laughed nervously. "Exactly."

I looked at him closely. Was there a nugget of truth in each of these accusations? It would make sense. Marla couldn't totally make these things up—I was pretty sure she didn't have an imagination. Lucinda sort of admitted that she slept her way to the top. And Cindy admitted to the liposuction. Without the internet, we couldn't prove she hadn't been married.

If Mitch had killed a guy and gotten away with it, it was certainly possible he was our killer here. Betty said he was a liar and that this charade with me was meant to distract me from his true purpose. But was that purpose to murder our classmates? Part of me hoped not because who wants a murderer flirting with them?

I turned back to the letter.

Veronica doesn't have a real estate license. She's been practicing without it. And she's actually the one who set fire to Lucinda's hair in chem. When Merry and Lucinda were looking the other way, I saw Veronica slide the burner closer to Lucinda!

"Hey, wait a minute…" I frowned. "I thought I…" my voice trailed off.

I reread the paragraph.

"I thought it was an accident?" Judy looked at me quizzically.

Lucinda turned to Veronica with murder in her eyes. "I thought so too."

"You did?" I asked. I'd always figured that the "accident" made Lucinda nicer to us.

"Of course! I knew it was an accident," Lucinda said to me before turning back to Veronica. "But I guess I was wrong."

Veronica seemed to turn green. "It's a lie! I swear it!"

"Which part?" Kelly asked. "You being a fraudulent real estate agent, or you setting Lucinda's hair on fire?"

"Both!" Veronica said a little hesitantly. "Of course I'm a licensed real estate agent! And I didn't move the burner!"

"Why would Marla say you did?" Judy asked. "She wasn't very imaginative. I can't see her making that up." She echoed my own thoughts.

Laughing, giggling Veronica had proven to be something rather different, from turning on me when Marla was murdered until now. It's interesting how you think you know the person who sold you your first house, only to find out that you really don't.

Which means that Veronica could've killed Marla to silence her. It may seem a bit extreme, but Veronica could lose all of her business if word got out. And she might get in serious trouble with the real estate agent governing association…if there was such a thing. I wasn't really sure about that. At any rate, people have killed for a lot less.

Once, there was this assassin for North Korea in Bogota. He moonlighted pretty much in the same field for extra money. He once killed a guy for a squirrel. The assassin and the squirrel, which he named Mr. Lumpy Foot, went on to have many adventures together and eventually retired to Gdansk—aka the Polish Riviera, where Mr. Lumpy Foot managed an umbrella kiosk. Why Lumpy Foot? I'm not entirely sure I translated it correctly. Korean is a bit different from Japanese, and it might have actually translated to Bumpy Noodle or Grumpy Pillow. I'm pretty sure it's Lumpy Foot though. Well, 80% sure.

"I don't know why she lied about me!" Veronica snapped. She was starting to come unglued.

"I think," Dylan said, "that she's half right. Like she was with Cindy and Mitch."

Ashley, Cindy, and Jason nodded while Mitch fumed.

We waited for Veronica to respond. You could practically see her weighing the consequences in her head as she wondered what she could get away with admitting to. I was a bit worried myself. If she wasn't a true real estate agent, did that mean my purchase of the house was illegitimate? I'd have to move all my stuff over to the other house, and that would suck. Rex didn't know about half the spy stuff I had. He'd probably make me throw out stuff, like the explosives.

Ashley said, "I think Lucinda at least deserves the truth. The real estate agent thing doesn't really affect any of us."

I spoke up. "Except for me. She sold me my house. If she's not licensed, does that mean the sale isn't legal?"

"Since the previous owner is dead"—Kelly rested her hand on my arm—"and you've lived there a few years, I doubt this changes anything."

Good. I really liked that house.

"I'm not addressing the slur against my professionalism," Veronica sniffed. "But I can see how Marla might've gotten the wrong idea about the burner. I was walking past the table where Lucinda and Merry were working, and I slipped, and to right myself, I accidentally grabbed the burner and slid it closer to Lucinda."

"You accidentally grabbed a hot burner and slid it closer to me?" Lucinda erupted, "Do you actually expect us to believe that? How could you?"

I didn't believe it. Why hadn't she grabbed at the table or Lucinda?

Veronica folded her arms over her chest and refused to say anything.

"This isn't over!" Lucinda held up her index finger. "When we're out of here, I'm going to investigate! You picked the wrong TV anchor to lie to!"

Okay. It seemed like this was a good time to get back to the speech.

Ashley and Amanda are the biggest frauds in our class! The twins were held back! Twice! They're actually two years older than us!

Some people blush. Others get a red creep that starts in their neck and floods their face. Ashley turned a rather alarming shade of deep purple.

"That's not so bad." Dylan put his arm around her. "Lots of people get held back for a number of reasons."

Kelly soothed, "It was your parents' decision. It probably had nothing to do with how smart you were."

She looked at Kelly and Dylan gratefully. "Unfortunately, it's true. I can't even blame late birthdays or overly cautious parents. We just weren't smart enough to start when we were five or six."

People murmured their support, and Ashley started to turn a lighter shade of mauve. She even kind of smiled. I had to wonder if people would've been as supportive if Marla had announced it. People could be cruel in a group setting, and there might have been laughter or snide comments. The humiliation would have been devastating to the twins.

"I'm glad Amanda wasn't here to see that. She'd probably kill Marla," Ashley said before bringing her hand to her mouth. "I mean, she didn't! It's just an expression!" She burst into tears.

Now that was interesting. Had Amanda killed Marla? That opened up a whole new realm of possibilities. If it was true, then did someone kill Amanda for revenge? And had she killed Barry too? I hadn't even thought of her as a suspect, mostly because she was dead.

"Let's move on," Dylan suggested.

I turned back to the speech.

Merry, or should I say Finn, has killed lots of people. And she and Kelly are probably lesbians.

"Huh." I leaned back in my chair. "I didn't see that coming."

"We're not lesbians," Kelly said calmly. "She must've thought so because we were always together."

Judy spoke up, "Marla never had a best friend. That makes sense."

"Marla never had any friends," Mitch said quietly. "She hung around with the popular kids, but none of us really liked her."

Lucinda agreed. "We never invited her to do anything one-on-one. Of course she hated people who had best friends."

Veronica snapped, "What about the other accusation? About Merry killing lots of people? It seems like this really implicates her in Marla's murder."

And we were back to that again.

"Merry was in the CIA," Mitch argued. "It's part of the job."

It was part of the job. I *had* killed people. But not *lots*. I mean, come on, lots implies dozens, right? Not that I didn't get blamed for killing some I technically didn't—like the one that I don't count because he backed into a moving truck while dancing out of my reach. That wasn't murder. It was just luck.

"She's exaggerating," I finally said. "I didn't kill lots of people when I was in the CIA."

"I'll bet you have some amazing stories." Mitch winked.

Judy, Cindy, Ashley, and Brandon leaned in hopefully. Kelly looked like she'd rather not know.

"Sorry," I apologized. "All of that is classified, and I'm not at liberty to discuss it." Hopefully, that would end it.

Veronica jumped to her feet. "So it's true! Which means you killed Marla! You should go to prison!"

"Technically," I began. "They were bad people and in other countries, so I wouldn't go to prison *here*."

"If you killed Marla, you'll go to prison here." Veronica folded her arms over her chest and glared at me.

Kelly waved for Veronica to sit back down. "Merry hasn't killed anyone since she got out."

"Um, thanks?"

"I'd know if she had," Kelly added. "And I'd turn her in if she'd murdered anyone."

I blinked at her. She would? Well, that hardly seemed best friend worthy. We'd have to have a chat about that later.

"Moving on." I read the next accusation.

Dylan is a drug dealer, and Judy is his biggest client!

Ashley turned to Dylan, eyebrows up. But she didn't exactly pull away from him. Maybe "drug dealer" wasn't as much of a dealbreaker to her.

"*Was*," Dylan insisted with steel in his voice. "I was dealing weed in high school. But I haven't since then."

"Was Judy your biggest client?" Cindy asked.

Judy spoke up. "I did smoke weed in high school. But I wasn't a total pot head." She squirmed in her seat, making me think there might be more to the story that she wasn't letting on. Like I'd mentioned earlier, we'd lost touch before middle school. I looked around to see the girls she hung with in high school, but those who had attended the reunion were passed out on the floor.

Dylan seemed uncomfortable. "Actually, Barry was my biggest client. And there was another one, but I don't want to say who it was since..."

"It was Amanda!" Judy blurted out. Within a few seconds, she seemed to regret what she'd said. Most likely because of Ashley's presence at the table.

Ashley's mouth dropped open as she stared at Judy. "What are you talking about?"

Dylan said, "Judy's right. I sold a lot of weed to your sister. I'm sorry."

"That's impossible." Ashley shook her head. "We were *twins*! How is it possible that I wouldn't know?"

Lucinda spoke up. "Well, you guys weren't exactly close."

This had the effect of a small bomb being dropped on the table—and as someone who's actually sat at a table when a small bomb was dropped on it, I'm not exaggerating when I say it makes a huge impact and was often very messy.

All through school, Amanda and Ashley had always seemed more like conjoined twins. They did everything together. Literally everything. At least, that's how it looked to me and everyone else.

"I didn't really want that out," Ashley said with irritation in her voice. "When you're twins, everyone expects you to be totally bonded. But as we grew older, we just developed different interests. Sure, we both work at the same store in the mall…" Ashley bit her lip but didn't correct *work* with *worked*. "But we just wanted to do separate things sometimes. Neither of us had a problem with that."

"But," Cindy said, "you guys were cheerleaders for football. You were both on the homecoming and prom courts. You were even lab partners in every class I had with you."

Ashley sighed. "I wasn't interested in those things. I really wanted to do theater and show choir. But Amanda thought it looked better if we were together in everything. And she was right back then. How many non-twin siblings get to do all the stuff we did?"

As an only child, I had no experience with that. Although I'd always imagined life with a sister would be one big bonding event. When I was four, I had an imaginary twin. Her name was Land. Considering that my name back then was Finn, I'll admit that it wasn't very imaginative. We went everywhere together, which wasn't difficult since Land existed in my head. She was vanquished from my life forever when I met Kelly. I guess I hadn't thought of her since. Huh. I wonder what she's been up to…

Ashley burst into tears. "What am I going to do without her? We may not have been close, but she was still a huge part of my life!"

Dylan pulled her against him, and she accepted gratefully. He looked like he'd just won the lottery, even though it had been due to a murder.

There was something interesting in what Dylan had said. He claimed that Barry and Amanda were his best clients. Was it just a coincidence that they were both dead? Had Dylan killed Marla, Barry, and Amanda to silence them about his past? I hadn't really considered him before. Which hardly seemed fair since he was just as likely to be the killer as anyone else.

"I've admitted to what Marla called me out on. I'm totally transparent about it. But this doesn't leave this table," Dylan pressed. "I'm starting a run for state senate. I'd never get it if they knew about this."

"You're running for public office?" Judy's jaw dropped.

"No one here has asked me what I do now." Dylan's eyes narrowed. "I'm an accountant. And I really wanted to shoot for the Iowa senate."

This only increased Dylan's motive in my mind. This was Iowa. People judged you on every little thing you did—especially in a small town. A drug-dealing past would crush a political career, even if it was when you were a kid.

"Okay." Mitch shrugged. "As long as none of this leaves the table, I'm okay with Dylan's druggie past."

Dylan glared at him but said nothing. The others more or less agreed to keep it to themselves. I did too, but if any of this was motive for murder, I would be telling the authorities about it once we were rescued.

"Keep going, Merry," Kelly urged. "I'm sure we all want this done as soon as possible."

It was surprising that I didn't have to skip around the speech much. It was as if Marla knew who would be discussing this and clumped us all together.

Kevin Dooley has a vicious, uncontrollable temper and almost killed Eddy Butz in eleventh grade! His dad got him out of trouble and somehow on the police force!

We all burst out laughing at once. The only emotion Kevin had was lethargy. His dad hadn't gotten him on the police force. But almost killed Eddy? Not only did he not have it in him, he'd be horribly inept at any attempt unless it involved food.

"It's true." Kevin scratched the side of his nose.

We stopped laughing.

I decided to clear this up. "You mean the part about your dad getting you out of trouble now and then."

He nodded. "That's true too."

Too? Kevin didn't seem to be affected by the accusation in any way. He looked just as dull-witted and unemotional as he always did.

"You tried to kill Eddy?" Ashley looked at the man on the floor. "Why?"

"How?" I had to ask.

Kevin shrugged. "He was mad about something. I was eating a cake. He took it and threw it against the wall. I threw him in a headlock. He almost died."

We stared at him.

He looked around the table. "What? I didn't *kill* him."

And then I remembered that Kevin once shot someone to save me. He did have it in him after all. Had he killed Marla for the cupcakes for Seamus's remembrance? I shook my head to clear it. No. It was impossible. While I could see Kevin attacking someone for destroying a cake (something I could relate to because cake is yummy), I couldn't see him killing anyone. Well, except for the guy he shot.

"Kevin?" Cindy said shakily as she pulled away.

He turned his sleepy gaze on her. "Yeah?"

"Barry was strangled," she said quietly.

His eyes widened. "He was? When?"

I relaxed. That was the Kevin Dooley I knew.

As Cindy gently reminded him, I looked at the speech. There wasn't anything on Brandon and Jason. I skimmed it just for names but never once came across theirs. I looked at them.

Jason asked, "Well? What does she say about me?"

Brandon glowered. "And me?"

I watched them carefully. "Nothing. Marla doesn't even mention you."

Brandon threw his hands in the air. "I can't even get a slam from the class monster!"

"Told you." Jason smiled. "I wasn't in the *in* crowd."

I cocked my head to the side. "You don't think it's weird that you two weren't mentioned?" I counted the other names on the list. "There are forty more names in this speech, and there are that many on the floor."

"Really?" Kelly counted the passed out classmates.

"She had a beef against everyone here?" Lucinda's eyes grew wide.

"Hold on," Judy protested. "There were a lot more in our class on the whole."

Kelly said, "Marla was on the reunion committee. She knew who was coming to the reunion. She might have just focused on the people who'd registered."

I wondered if she had something planned for those who weren't here. Was she going to mail them a letter? Show up on their doorstop to accuse them of something sinister? I wouldn't think that would go over well.

"So that's it for everyone here?" Mitch tapped the piece of paper in my hands.

I pulled the speech to my chest so that no one would read the rest of it like we'd agreed. "That's it."

Judy frowned and looked at Jason and Brandon. "Which again begs the question, if Marla planned to air dirty laundry on everyone here, why aren't you two slammed?"

Brandon shouted, "Because for some reason, no one remembers me!"

"It's just a theory," Jason said amiably, "that she wrote up something on everyone. We don't have proof of that."

"So," Lucinda sounded exasperated. "Are we any closer to finding out who killed Marla, Barry, and Amanda?"

"I think so," Ashley said. "Mitch, Kevin, and Merry have killed before. Which puts them at the top of the list of suspects."

Cindy spoke up, "Leave Merry out of it! She didn't do it!"

Everyone began speaking at once, each accusing the others of murder. I didn't really care. I knew I was innocent. I started to read the rest of the speech, hoping the others wouldn't notice. I know we said we weren't going to read aloud the accusations against those who couldn't defend themselves. But maybe there was a clue in here to Amanda's and Barry's murders.

"Mrs. Wrath!" Lauren called out from the stage. "Caterina found something!"

I folded the speech and shoved it into my bra for later, left the table of my bickering classmates, and trotted across the gym to the girls.

Caterina was staring intently at something on the stage floor.

"What is it?" I said as I jumped up beside her.

Embedded in between two planks was a garrote made of fishing line, with two leather bits on each end for holding it.

"Here." Betty handed me two pencils.

Using the pencils like chopsticks, I picked up the garrote and held it in the air. I pulled the speech out and only half unfolded it, laying the garrote in the fold.

"A garrote." Betty stared at it. "Probably the one that killed that one guy."

"Maybe," I hedged. "It certainly looks like it."

"What if it isn't?" Ava asked.

Everyone was running so roughshod over the truth that I didn't want to add to the fearmongering by deciding this was the murder weapon. "I don't know what it's doing here, unless it's a prop in a school play."

"How will we know?" Lauren asked.

"Forensic testing," I said. "There aren't any hairs or pieces of skin. But there'd be tiny skin cells. And maybe fingerprints on the leather."

Betty shook her head at the weapon. "Mine's bigger."

I wouldn't be surprised in the least.

CHAPTER SIXTEEN

I folded the garrote into the speech and stuffed it into my pocket, giving a silent thanks that the world's most uncomfortable dress at least had pockets. It didn't seem like the right time to announce that we might have the weapon that killed Barry. From the escalating shouting across the gym, the most important thing would be to diffuse the furious attacks being screamed from every side.

The only one who didn't seem bothered was Kevin, who was scooping microscopic crumbs off the table into his hand. He tilted his head back and dumped whatever was in his fist into his mouth.

"Want me to break this up?" Betty asked as she held up a fire extinguisher.

"Yes and no," I answered. "Let's go with no." Spraying my classmates with chemicals was unlikely to calm things down.

Betty looked disappointed. "Come on. It would be a great chance to try out my defusing an angry mob skills."

The other girls nodded.

It was tempting. And that defusing an angry mob thing did sound legitimate. I'd have to look into that training once we got out. "No. Better not. This is keeping them busy, which is a good thing."

Kelly extricated herself from the table and walked over. "Well, they're wearing themselves out."

Lauren nudged her and out of the corner of her mouth said, "We found the thing that killed the guy."

I explained and pulled the garrote from my pocket, displaying it on the folded-up speech.

"Do you think it's the murder weapon?" Her eyes grew wide.

"It could be." I shrugged.

"Why aren't you sure?" Kelly pressed. "I mean, how often do you find a weapon like that on a high school stage?"

It was a good point, and I was about to say so when a paper plate came whizzing between us. The shouting had turned into an all-out brawl.

"Are you sure?" Betty held up the fire extinguisher. "It'll only hurt for a few seconds."

Kelly took the fire extinguisher. "It doesn't hurt."

"It does the way I do it," Betty responded.

"Yes," I said. "I'm absolutely sure."

"Okay," Betty said before she put her fingers in her mouth and whistled.

It worked better than spraying them. Everyone froze as the shrill whistle bounced off the walls. They looked around, blinking—as if they had no idea what they'd been doing.

"Guys!" I said as I joined the group. "We don't have much longer till the janitor lets us out. We need to stop fighting."

Kelly added, "Let's take a little break. We're all tired. There's a stack of mats by the boys' locker room. You can sit wherever you want, as long as you stay in groups and we can all see each other."

Dylan and Ashley grabbed a mat and went over to a corner. They sat and leaned against the wall, with Ashley's head on Dylan's shoulder.

Jason and Brandon each grabbed a mat and moved to the other side of the boys' locker room door. They didn't unfold their mats, but lay down on them and closed their eyes. Those two had stuck to each other all night. They didn't seem to know each other eleven years ago, but now they were always together. It didn't help that my spydy senses seemed to go off when I looked at Brandon—although that could just be recognition. There were moments when his voice or mannerisms seemed a bit familiar to me. Which, if true, meant that I did recognize him from all those years ago. But even so, even if he did go to school with me, he still could be a murderer. He was certainly angry enough.

Were Jason and Brandon working together to murder my classmates? I couldn't shake off the suspicion that something was off about them. And then there was the fact that Marla didn't name them in her live or written speech. That couldn't just be coincidence.

How could I find out more? Both men had clammed up. We didn't have internet access, so I couldn't check them out online. Our questioning of them hadn't gone well. And they were both kind of hostile to the rest of us. Brandon was spitting mad all the time, and even though Jason was calm, there was a seething quality to him just beneath the surface.

And what did we really know about the others? We only had their word for it that they were telling the truth. The accusation against Mitch really bothered me. I wasn't sure if it was because he'd been flattering me with his attention all night, or if my sixth sense was telling me he really had killed that guy.

In my experience as an amateur sleuth, and from being married to a detective, people killed for many reasons, but emotion was a big factor. When emotions run high, people drop their inhibitions and the line between right and wrong. It's why it's called a crime of passion. What was it in Marla's speech that could've induced that?

The accusations seemed severe in some cases and ridiculous in others. Like Kelly and me probably being lesbians. That was laughable. But there were two accusations lobbied against me, and the other one was true. Marla seemed to riddle her slams with truth, peppered with unproven claims.

My classmates reacted to the charges in different ways. Lucinda laughed and admitted it. Cindy didn't get mad. She just pointed out what was true and what was not. Ashley was embarrassed by her revelation. Mitch seemed worried and angry at the same time. I needed to try to get to the bottom of that one. Dylan and Judy admitted to part of the allegations leveled against them. And Veronica…she straight up lost her mind. That was interesting.

Marla wanted to strike back at all of us who'd somehow slighted her eleven years ago. These slanders were meant to wound deeply, so if she'd been alive to carry them out, she'd probably be disappointed in our reactions. Most of these people shrugged it off. But Veronica had not. She went absolutely scorched earth on me. My real estate agent, who may not be a real real estate agent, deflected her anger to me. Why? Was that a way for her to deal with what Marla had said? I needed to check that out and looked around to locate the woman.

I found Veronica sitting with Judy in the bleachers between the two locker rooms, talking in low voices. I wasn't sure, but I got the impression that Judy was trying to calm Veronica down. That was good. If I was going to get more information out of her, I'd need to make it seem like that wasn't my goal. She would need to be calm when I questioned her. In fact, I'd have to sympathize with her, and it wouldn't be easy to do that when she thought I'd killed Marla. Of course, if she'd killed Marla, then she'd know I wasn't guilty. If that was the case, I was going to have to approach it very, very carefully. Maybe I'd have Betty with a fire extinguisher on standby just to be safe.

Kelly was trying to get the girls to nap out on a series of mats she'd set up on the opposite side of the gym. They weren't having it. I recognized those stubborn attitudes. They were hopped up on the adrenaline of three murders. Kelly needed assistance. I was about to go over when Mitch appeared at my side, holding up a mat and wiggling his eyebrows suggestively.

"Not a chance," I said.

I started to walk over to my troop, but Kelly shook her head, most likely indicating that my presence would make things worse. And since it wasn't the first time that had happened, I changed course and joined Lucinda and Cindy, who were sitting in the bleachers, glumly staring into space. Kevin was stretched out on one of the bleacher benches a few rows behind them, eyes closed and probably sleeping. Mitch dragged his mat over to Jason and Brandon and followed their lead by going to sleep.

"How are you guys holding up?" I asked as I sat down between them.

"I really believed it was an accident," Lucinda said sadly. "Why would Veronica want to set fire to my hair?"

I was still shocked that Lucinda hadn't thought I'd done it on purpose for all these years. But hey, when you get an opportunity like this, you grab it and run.

"She's acting weird," I said. "For the past few years, every time I talked to her, she was bursting with giggle fits."

Cindy spread her hands open. "I haven't seen any of you since high school. I have no idea if anyone is acting differently."

I had few answers. "Well, I for one believe it. Who stumbles and reaches for an open flame to stop their fall when they could've just grabbed the table? That doesn't make sense." I thought back to the moment in question and was transported back in time to the chemistry room. Looking around the scene, something hit me. "Now that I think about it, I do remember Veronica walking by when it happened. But I don't recall her stumbling. That would've gotten our attention."

"But why did Veronica do it?" Lucinda pressed her original question.

"Maybe she was jealous of you?" I suggested. "You were certainly more popular than her. And prettier."

Looking across the gym, I noticed that Veronica was relaxing. Good job, Judy.

Cindy added, "And you were dating Mitch." She looked at me strangely. "I had no idea you two were dating, though."

"About that." Lucinda seemed a bit confused. "I didn't know either."

I explained. "That's because it didn't happen. It's pure fiction."

Lucinda continued on, "I don't remember him ever mentioning you, except to call you the weird girl."

"Weird girl?" Well, I was kind of weird. For a teenager to keep to the shadows probably did seem odd at an age when kids took whatever notoriety they could get.

"He would say 'there goes that weirdo who didn't let me cut in line in the lunchroom.'" Lucinda appeared to be in a fog of nostalgia.

I held up my hands. "I get it. Yes, that proves that we didn't have a thing back then."

But she didn't seem to hear me. "Or check out that kook who got an A+++ on her paper on the Cold War."

"Okay," I laughed it off. "You proved your point."

I really did get teased for getting an A with three pluses on it. Mr. Melborne held it up and showed the whole class, saying this was how it's done. Marla had accused me of getting help from my dad, but I hadn't.

"And then there was the time when he said you were always mooning over him in English…"

I clapped my hands to break her out of her reverie. "I get it. I was weird. Let's move on."

A look of horror came over Lucinda's pretty features. "I'm sorry! I shouldn't have said those things! Really, Merry, I just got carried away."

"It's okay." I ignored Cindy struggling not to laugh out loud. "Actually, those things prove what I've been saying all night about Mitch—that he never so much as talked to me back then."

"Maybe he was disguising his feelings for you by insulting you?" Lucinda offered.

I shook my head. "I don't think so. You've helped me. Now I have more ammo to confront him with."

I looked at the three men who appeared to be fast asleep. "Did any of you know about the guy Marla said he killed in Waterloo?"

Cindy shook her head, but Lucinda's eyes lit up with recognition.

"I was a reporter in Cedar Falls. I covered the story. It was suspicious because Mitch was the only one on that floor with…I think his name was Danielson. Anyway, one of the witnesses below swore he saw Mitch looking over the edge of the scaffolding right after Danielson hit the ground."

"Mitch said he didn't do it," I said.

"Other witnesses insisted that they didn't see Mitch looking over," Lucinda continued. "But both of them worked for Mitch, so it's hard to say if they were telling the truth."

Cindy thought about this. "He could be our killer. Maybe he knew Marla was going to dredge that up."

"But why kill Barry and Amanda?" Lucinda asked.

"Maybe Barry saw him kill Marla," I offered. "Or Mitch thought he saw him. Mitch would be strong enough to strangle someone quickly."

I decided not to bring out the garrote just yet.

Cindy nodded. "Makes sense. But why Amanda?"

"I don't know. All of our suspects seem to be logical for one or two of the murders—not all three. Except for Dylan." I explained my idea on that one.

Cindy tsked. "That would be too bad. He really seems to be helping Ashley."

Lucinda nodded. "He's comforting for her. Imagine losing your sister."

"You said they weren't that close," I interjected. "What's up with that?"

"I feel bad about bringing that up." Lucinda blushed. "Amanda was the star. She was popular and funny, outgoing and smart. Everybody loved her and just took on Ashley because of her sister. They didn't have a lot in common. I was more Ashley's friend than Amanda's. But Ashley kept up appearances. I think she was dazzled by her twin. Like a younger sibling worshiping an older one."

Cindy shook her head sadly. "I guess the only good thing to come out of that is that Ashley will get more of the spotlight now."

Lucinda disagreed, "Oh, I think she'd hate it. Amanda overshadowed her, but she liked that. And when people wanted the twins to do something, Ashley could beg off as long as Amanda went. I think it will be hard on her."

We sat in silence for a moment. Everyone on a mat on the gym floor seemed to be passed out, except for Kelly, who was keeping a close eye on the girls. They looked like they were asleep, but my troop were experts in subterfuge. During sleepovers, I often had to stay up all night to make sure they weren't raiding the fridge, going on a nighttime hike, or putting Betty's oft mentioned plan of kidnapping the mayor, for no apparent reason, into action. I wondered if she'd stop bringing up that idea once Ava was mayor.

Cindy finally broke the silence. "Don't you think it's bizarre how easily all the men can sleep at a time like this?"

She wasn't wrong. While the women were still awake, all of the men were out cold.

"Men are strange," I said. "What I can't believe is that our classmates are still passed out on the floor."

I really needed to know how Betty pulled off the sleeping binge after an LSD bender. It could come in useful when Randi and Ronni, my sisters-in-law, came by. I'd only use it on Ronni because she hates me. Like really, really hates me. Of course, I'd have to come up with a reason why Rex's sister was passed out on the living room floor...

Lucinda nodded, but neither she nor Cindy commented. They were starting to stare off into space again. I would love to do that too. Just tune all of this out and think of other things. In a situation like this, it would be like a restful nap.

Hopefully, soon, the night janitor would show up and release us. My goal was to ride out the rest of the time so that no one else ended up dead. It was a crapshoot. I still wasn't sure who the killer was. Oh, I had my suspicions, but things weren't clear.

Did I really need to solve this before we could summon the authorities? We could just all sit here, keeping an eye on one another, until the calvary came. It seemed pretty conceited of me to want to solve this. Was I trying to help or just seeking the approval of my classmates? If the latter, that wasn't the best reason to solve a murder...or three.

I rubbed my face to get the blood circulating. When I looked over at Kelly, she gave me a thumbs-up to indicate that she'd actually gotten the girls to go to sleep. Or at least, pretend they were. I nodded at her. My co-leader wasn't going to let anything happen to those girls.

What was my plan of action here—sit tight and wait for our way out? What if the killer struck again? I'd been looking for bits of connectivity to the murders, but if this was a spree killing, I might never be able to figure out why these three people were killed.

Something inside me said Marla was killed for being a nasty piece of work. But the others? If she was poisoned by her inhaler, then Amanda's murder was premeditated. Which meant the killer had struck before the party even started or had brought the poisoned inhaler to make the switch at the party. The spree killer theory didn't seem to work with Amanda's murder, but I could be wrong.

What about Barry? My mind reeled back to when we found him dead. I'd been backstage with pretty much everyone else. What happened before he was killed? There'd been absolute chaos on the gym floor, and the others had made their way to the stage. I missed some of that, and then they passed out.

Was it possible that Barry was strangled during the LSD freak out? The killer could've done it right in front of everyone, and people might not have noticed with all hell breaking loose. The killer could've walked around the gym floor inconspicuously.

The LSD trip was an absolute gift to the killer. The girls had inadvertently provided the opportunity to kill Barry. It wasn't their fault. Well, it was their fault, and tomorrow I was going to get hold of Hilly if I had to fly to Peru. The CIA assassin (who wasn't an assassin) had messed up this time. Her indulgence of a group of eleven-year-olds was bad news.

A thought struck me. Had another classmate, whacked out of their mind on LSD, strangled Barry because they thought that he was an attacking tiger? A homicidal maniac? A thirty-foot tall pterodactyl with paper airplanes for hands and a penchant for singing Barry Manilow songs? Oh wait, that last one was mine.

The CIA dosed us on one occasion during training right after I'd seen *Jurassic Park*. My alarm clock back then played Barry Manilow for reasons I couldn't explain. I think my old friend Maria had played a joke on me, and I was never able to change it. The thought made me sad.

I missed my old friend, but she'd defected from the CIA and gone off the grid after accusing them of having too much power. Maybe Hilly's seen her! We could set up a girls' weekend in Ecuador or Belize when this was over!

But first I had to get through this night without another murder. My thoughts rolled back to wondering about the order of the deaths. It seemed important to sort that out. It might be the key to the whole thing.

Maybe Amanda was the primary target—the killer just hadn't switched the inhalers before they decided to off Marla and, later, Barry. That would shake up the order of the killings and throw out a number of motives. If the killer came here planning to kill Amanda and, after hearing her speech, decided to kill Marla, then I had to rethink the timeline.

Someone had tried to kill me when they cut the rope I was climbing down on. But that seemed more reactionary and less like I was a target. Or it was a distraction to draw attention away from Barry's murder.

And then there was the attempt on Kelly. Something about that was off. I wasn't sure why, but it felt like that wasn't a true murder attempt. I couldn't put my finger on it, but it seemed like a red herring—or a warning.

Why would anyone attack Kelly? She was the nice, mature one of the two of us. And she wasn't pressing everyone into figuring out who the killer was. That was me. Why didn't they attack me again?

Opportunity, for one. Kelly had been sitting at the table, and I was out wandering around in the dark. It would have been harder to pin me down for a strike. If my theory that it was a warning was correct, did that mean the killer might take it one step further and attack one of the girls? My stomach roiled. That could not happen. The killer needed to be unmasked.

There I was again, trying to solve this. What else was I going to do? I had to stay awake to make sure the killer didn't strike again. But without looking like I was waiting for the killer to strike again. That made sense…maybe only to me.

"…and then he married Heather," Cindy was saying. "Which destroyed his best friend."

"I'm sorry, guys," I interrupted. "What's going on?"

"We're just gossiping." Lucinda smiled. "That's what you do at reunions, right?"

"I have no idea," I admitted. "But I'm pretty sure you don't kill off your classmates. That doesn't seem right."

Cindy and Lucinda smiled in spite of all this.

"There's really not a lot that's happened in ten…I mean eleven years," Cindy said.

I waved my hand up and down at her. "Lucinda may still look like she did when we graduated, but you've totally changed in that time." I looked around the gym. "Most people have. I mean some have gained or lost weight…"

"Or lost hair," Cindy said.

"Or classmates." Lucinda bit her lip. "Poor Seamus. It really was tragic."

I really didn't want to go there. "I wonder why Marla wanted to honor his memory. It doesn't seem like her to do that."

The other women frowned as they thought about that.

"It really was uncharacteristic," Cindy agreed. "I'm surprised she didn't have a documentary about her own life."

"Ugh." Lucinda grimaced. "I'd have killed her to stop her from doing that."

There was an awkward silence.

"But I didn't," she added quickly.

"It's okay," I sighed. "Remember, I said I wished a two-ton weight would fall on her, and I didn't kill her."

"You could have," Cindy pondered. "I don't mean any offence of course, but think about it. You could be leading the investigation just to throw us off you being the killer."

"You'd know how to strangle Barry and poison Amanda." Lucinda nodded.

Cindy agreed as they both looked at me.

"But I didn't," I insisted. Was that what my classmates thought of me? That I might be the killer? That would suck.

"We're just worn out and throwing out wild theories," Cindy assured me. "I'm convinced you didn't do it, Merry."

Lucinda seemed to agree. "Me too."

I relaxed a bit. "I know that. We're just getting punchy."

My mind went back to the strange notion of Marla doing a memorial to Seamus. She'd made cupcakes with little tombstones on them. That was in poor taste, not that someone like Marla cared.

"Classic narcissistic psychology. She did it to get more attention for herself," Kevin said from the bleacher bench above us. He was still on his back with his eyes closed, and I could swear he was snoring.

I waited for more, but he issued no further statement. It took me ten whole seconds to force my jaw shut.

"He's right," Cindy said. "Kevin has remarkable insight into the human condition, doesn't he? It must be part of his police training."

The old Merry would've said something snarky. But the new Merry was slightly impressed. And she was going to keep that to herself.

"What a sick way to steal the spotlight." Lucinda seemed disgusted. "Seamus was a great guy. I'm sure Barry, Eddy, Mitch, and the rest of the football team miss him." She paused. "Well, not Barry. Barry isn't missing anything but his own life."

"Marla really was a piece of work. Excuse me." I got up and walked down the bleachers and over to Kelly.

"You missed it," I said as I plopped down next to her. "Kevin said something intelligent. In his sleep no less."

Kelly nodded. "I think there's potential in there somewhere."

My jaw dropped. "You do?"

She nodded. "I do. Why not? People change."

"I haven't changed."

Kelly looked me in the eye. "Yes, you have. You were a spy with a carefree life and no attachments. Now you're a Girl Scout leader with an amazing husband."

"Huh," I mused. "I hadn't thought about it like that."

"Change is unavoidable," Kelly continued. "It's been ten, I mean eleven years. Time to cut Kevin some slack."

An unformed idea popped into my head. "Kelly, do you think Marla, Barry, and Amanda were killed because they'd changed?"

She frowned. "What do you mean?"

I shrugged because I wasn't sure myself. "Maybe the three of them changed, which upset the killer? Most people don't handle change well."

I knew this from experience. As a spy, your environment, personality, appearance, and even address changed regularly, and it was a unique individual who handled it well. One example in particular was a guy named Wilbur, who was in my graduating class at the CIA. Wilbur breezed through training. He even excelled at his first field assignment in Paraguay. It was the second assignment where things began to turn bad.

When he went to Estonia, he couldn't remember his new cover. He even spoke in Spanish the whole time, which, in

Estonia, really makes you stand out. Riley was handling him then and pulled him from the case, even sending him home.

Within a year he'd washed out of the agency and decided to move back to Paraguay, resuming his cover as a vacuum cleaner salesman. Of course a CIA cover is totally fiction, and he sold a few machines before he realized they were props, and he wasn't getting paid anyhow because the company he worked for never existed. Hilly ran into him a year ago in Asuncion, where he was working as a street mime. It's kind of funny how he went from one imaginary job to another.

"If that was true, he'd want to kill everyone here," Kelly continued. "Because all of us are different now. Haven't you noticed how no one is really hanging around in their old cliques? Judy and Veronica weren't friends in high school. Cindy and Lucinda probably never said one word to each other back then. And Mitch didn't know you were alive."

"And then there's Jason and Brandon—who no one remembers." I looked at the sleeping girls. "I need to see those yearbooks."

"I don't get it." Kelly looked puzzled. "Why would they be here if they didn't go to school with us?"

That was the part that tripped me up. "I'm not sure I'm saying that neither one of them went to school with us. One of them, maybe. If whoever that is saw this as an opportunity, why not?"

"But that doesn't explain Amanda's murder. If she was poisoned through her inhaler, the killer had to do that in advance. I can believe it if it was just Marla and Barry. But Amanda doesn't make sense."

I was exhausted. My brain hurt. "I'm going to walk around. If I bring you those yearbooks, can you see if you recognize our Brandon and Jason with the Brandons and Jasons in the yearbooks?"

Kelly agreed. "And if it isn't them?"

"Then it could be anyone." I sighed. "At least I know it's not you or the girls or Kevin."

She cocked her head to one side. "You don't think it's Kevin?"

"You do?" I asked. "You just said we should cut him some slack!"

"Not if he's the killer." Kelly shifted on the mat. "Go get the yearbooks."

I did as I was told and began walking laps around the gym, being careful not to step on those who were reclined and those who were knocked out…and those who were dead. Everyone else slept or chatted quietly.

Movement helped. The blood started flowing, and my head cleared a little. I tried not to think about the situation and let my mind go blank. Have you ever tried that? It's almost impossible. When I'd compartmentalize one thing, five more would spring up in its place.

I just couldn't get a handle on it. Granted, you usually find the motive when you figure out who the killer was. In my experience, you could do it the other way around, find the motive and then the killer. But figuring out the killer first usually worked best.

And in a situation where you had three people dead—whose only connection is that they went to high school together, it's tough. Add to that fact that there were multiple possibilities for the killer, and I needed a drink.

I stopped at the bar, thanking the passed out bartender who lay nearby. I found a half bottle of cheap wine. Huh. All the bottles were cheap. Marla must've decided to go cheap. I hated her all over again.

No, if I was going to keep my wits about me, drinking wine probably wasn't the best idea. I found a can of generic cola and started drinking that. How long had it been since I'd eaten? My stomach rumbled an answer. There was no way I was going to "Kevin" it out by eating napkins.

You know, I'd been all over this gym, and I couldn't figure out how the killer had eluded us this entire time. Let alone go in and out of the gym unnoticed. Why wouldn't we see that? It made me feel like an idiot, which, to be fair, I kind of was.

I paused in front of Ashley and Dylan, who were sound asleep. The killer could've gotten around by using keys, and these two had refused to empty their pockets and purse to prove they weren't the killer. Her purse was lying about a foot away from her, just off the mat. Maybe I should take a look.

Dylan shifted, rolling over and putting his arm over Ashley, his hand resting on the purse. It was still tempting. The problem would be if I got caught. I don't know what would happen, but it wouldn't be pretty.

And what if I found something? I could put it back and find a way of cajoling her to open her purse. I couldn't guarantee it though, and it seemed a little mean to do that to her.

Another thought popped into my mind. What if Dylan and Ashley were working together? What if they'd known each other before tonight and set the whole thing up?

That changed everything. I bent down and reached for the purse.

CHAPTER SEVENTEEN

I had just touched the strap when Ashley began crying softly in her sleep. I took a few steps backward as Dylan woke up. He didn't seem to see me at all, just rubbed Ashley's arm until the tears stopped.

This was an interesting theory. Dylan admitted that he had something to lose if word got out about his past occupation. Did he know Marla was going to do this ahead of time, or did he figure it out when she gave her first speech? Maybe he broke the ladder when he climbed up onto the catwalk. He wasn't that heavy, but heavier than me.

Where was he during the class LSD trip? I had been so preoccupied with finding out if Marla's murder was an accident, I hadn't counted the folks who were backstage. He could've killed Barry, gotten up to the roof to cut the rope, and then returned and locked us all in again.

Unfortunately, this scenario could apply to almost everyone here. I remembered Cindy being backstage with the girls the whole time. And Mitch was there when I fell. I couldn't be sure where the others were. There were a lot of us backstage.

This was getting me nowhere. I stopped and tugged on my dress again. Why hadn't I worn jeans like most of the guys? This dress was no good for something like this. Of course, I had no idea that I'd be dealing with murder when I got dressed.

If I kept going through theories in my head, I'd lose my mind. I needed to *do* something productive, but what? I'd explored the dressing room beneath the stage and the catwalk over it. Standing in front of the girls' locker room, I wondered if I should give it another once-over. After counting the men in the gym to avoid any surprises in the toilet stalls, I went in.

I never liked the locker room. Maybe that was because I wasn't a jock. Gym class either bored, confused, or terrified me. It probably was the same for most people.

"Hello?" I called out softly, just to make sure.

No one answered. I wasn't really sure what I was doing in there in the first place, but I figured I'd know it if I found it. Was all police work like that? You didn't know what you had until you found the weapon or the suspect or the victim? I'd have to ask Rex about it if I got out of here alive.

The thought was jarring, but who knew who the killer would target next? Kelly's attack had been a surprise, but I couldn't shake the feeling that the killer wasn't planning to kill her. This whole thing was so confusing. Perhaps that was the point? Confusion?

Thinking of it that way, I could see how the next victim could be me as much as anyone else. Coming in here alone may not have been the brightest idea. But I was pretty sure Kelly had seen me come in and would notice someone else going in after me.

Then again, she was on yearbook duty and may not have even noticed. Should I go back out and tell her? Or would that advertise to the killer, *Hey, look over here! I'm in here all alone!* He or she had tried to kill me already by cutting the rope. Why not just finish me off?

Great. I was psyching myself out. Which is a terrible thing for a spy to do. In the field, I would be so focused on whatever my assignment was that I didn't have time to worry about things like this. I was getting rusty. I needed to approach this like I did back then.

Right. I'm looking for something. I don't know what, but I'll know when I find it. After all, I found...well, Betty found Marla's speech. I patted my pocket just to make sure it was still there.

Right inside the door from the gym were two rows of lockers, facing each other and connected at the wall. I'd start with those. Most of the lockers had padlocks on them. Since I didn't have time to pick them, I'd have to assume that those belonged to students. The killer could've brought their own padlock, but I'd never know which one it was, and there had to be fifty lockers in here.

A few were open, so I searched. After all, the lockers were the closest to the gym, and the killer could stash something here easily without raising too much suspicion. Everyone here had gone in and out of this door at some point tonight.

The unlatched lockers were void of anything. I carefully ran my hands over the insides, looking for something taped to them, but all I found was one marijuana joint. I doubted it was the killer's, so I put it back. There was no way I was getting involved in another crime by turning in some poor kid.

On the other side of the lockers, along each wall, were showers on the left, toilet cubicles on the right, with two long benches down the middle and sinks at the far end. The door to the hallway was in the left corner.

I started with the toilets, checking behind and under each one. The back of the doors had posters about feminine hygiene and an upcoming dance. Carefully, I peeled back the tape on each one on the off chance the killer had slid something in there.

To be honest, I felt a little ridiculous. Besides Marla's speech, what could the killer hide in here? I'd found the garrote...a garrote on the stage. What was I going to find? A note that said, *Good job! I'm the killer!* signed with block letters so that I'd be able to read it easily?

Now that I thought about it, it would be nice to have that. Oh well. At least the benches, sinks, and showers would be easier to search.

There was a sound. A soft scrape that sounded like the door was closing. Hopefully, it was a woman. I opened my mouth to speak, but something inside my head told me to close it. Very slowly, I climbed on top of a toilet and waited, with my knees drawn up in front of me.

My spydy senses were tingling. If something happened, I just needed to scream and half the gym would come running to my rescue. Maybe even Mitch, if he wasn't the killer. Eeew— what if he followed me in here for some "alone time"?

I'd break all of his fingers.

There was no other sound. Perhaps no one had come in—they just closed the door. Or they were just inside the door, listening for me. Good luck, I thought. I was very good at being quiet. No one would hear me if I didn't want them to.

There was a brief shuffling sound near the door that I couldn't decipher. Someone was in here with me. Then I heard the door swing open and close again. My heart started pounding. Was it the killer? Had he or she snuck in to retrieve something or hide it? And I missed it?

Hope rose in my heart, but I stayed right where I was. And I waited for at least five minutes. Nobody was in here with me. That was good. I was just starting to straighten my legs when the lights went out.

Have you ever gone from overhead fluorescent lighting to total darkness? It's really quite disabling, and the darkness is all-encompassing. I sat there, confused for a second, before I heard the stall door slam open and a pair of hands dragged me out.

I fought back and started to cry out, but a towel was wrapped around my mouth. I silently prayed it was a clean one. Both of my arms were sharply drawn back and together, and I felt them being tied. I kicked behind me and connected with a leg. There was an *oof*, but that was it. I couldn't tell if it was male or female.

Dropping to the floor, I escaped my captor's grip. If someone is trying to kidnap you off the street, go limp and fall to the ground. Standing up, your efforts to struggle are used against you to help propel you into the back of a van, a car with tinted windows, or one time in Moldova—an ox cart. If you go limp, you're dead weight. They are forced to pick you up. All of you.

Lying on my back I lashed out with both feet, managing to hit the person at least once. I couldn't call out because of the hopefully fresh from the laundry towel. I couldn't see, so I had no idea who my attacker was. There wasn't any way to tell if it was even a man or woman or, like the time in Moldova, a gigantic goatherd named Steve who spied for the Russians.

The pair of hands found my arms and yanked hard until I was sitting upright, my back to the bench. I heard the snick of metal as I was cuffed to the bench leg.

I heard footsteps moving toward the door to the gym, then the gym door close, then…someone turning a key in the lock. Then nothing.

I was locked inside a dark locker room, blindfolded, gagged, and handcuffed to a bench. I'd come in here looking for something that may not have even existed and gave the killer the opportunity to lock me up.

A thought occurred to me. The killer hadn't finished me off. Was it because I was fighting too hard? Did they lose their nerve? Or had they just hoped to get me away from the action?

Sooner or later, someone would do a head count and realize I was missing. But what good would that do if the door was locked? And was the killer right now taking out another one of my classmates?

I screamed into the towel and writhed, straining against the cuffs. After a few moments of that unhelpful behavior, I panted and gathered my thoughts. How was the killer able to see in the dark? How did they know exactly where I was? Maybe I wasn't as quiet as I'd thought.

Well, this was a nightmare I was living out in reality—one of my classmates was trying to kill me in the girls' locker room.

Okay, enough of the defeatist thinking. I had to get out of this situation. I've always found, when bound, gagged, and blindfolded in a dark, locked room (and yes, this has happened to me—three times, actually), that the best way to approach the situation is bit by bit. One thing at a time.

Going for the gag made sense because then I could shout and warn the others. But how to get it off? I brought my knees up as close to my face as I could, but since I had the flexibility of a two-by-four, I couldn't get close enough. Removing the blindfold, while making me more comfortable, would do nothing because the room was already pitch black.

I'd like to tell you that my other senses were heightened in this light-deprived situation (because that would be awesome), but I'd be lying. The fact of the matter was, I was no Houdini. However, I was resourceful. Now, how could I make that work for me?

After feeling around behind me with my fingers, I discovered that my hands were tied with rope, and the rope was handcuffed to the bench. My attacker hadn't had enough time to properly cuff me to the post. That was a relief because working my way out of ropes *and* handcuffs was a little too much to ask of me at the moment.

As my hands worked the knot, my mind wondered who had handcuffs, and for a second, my fingers froze. The only person I knew, who was here, with handcuffs was Kevin Dooley.

Was Kevin the killer?

CHAPTER EIGHTEEN

No! I refused to believe it. Kevin had the intelligence of a fruit fly, and he had nothing against me. Sure, it would be a solid reason why he hadn't killed me, since I am his boss's wife and all. But was Kevin capable of such things? Had Kevin finally snapped?

People are strange creatures. Sometimes you can go your entire life thinking you know someone, only to find out that you really don't. Case in point, for a classified amount of time in Colombia, when I was embedded with Carlos the Armadillo, Riley and I worked with a woman named Tamar. She was shy, quiet, and friendly. We really liked her. She gave us absolutely no indication that there was an issue—until the day she took off all her clothes, painted her arms and legs yellow, and ran out onto the soccer field at a World Cup match.

At first, I thought maybe she was showing some team spirit with that color. But no. She ran onto the field, stole the ball, and proceeded to eat it. We later found out that the real Tamar had never made it down to Colombia, and this woman, an escaped lunatic, had taken her place because we'd mistaken her for a colleague we'd never met.

It was a shock, but not a total loss. That woman could bake. She made the best pineapple upside-down cake I'd ever had. Oh well. *Comme çi, comme ça.* Whatever that means.

The point is, was I wrong about Kevin Dooley? Could he have been a psycho killer all along, and we just didn't know? Or was his behavior triggered by the fact that the food had run out? He had said something completely out of character in the bleachers not long ago. What if food was the only thing that kept a psycho complacent? The whole time I'd known him, he was always eating. Always.

Ugh! How was this helping me? One thing at a time, I thought to myself. I needed to focus on the ropes. Then take off the blindfold and gag. Then turn on the lights and bust out of this room so that I could hunt Kevin Dooley for sport. Maybe I could find a jar of paste and use it as a lure.

My fingers worked the knot until it started to loosen, then finally pulled free. I was free from the cuffs and removed the towels from my face. Nope. Still couldn't see a thing.

I remembered the layout of the room. Getting to my feet, I stood up and reached out, my hands brushing against the toilet stall door on my left. Okay. I was facing the right direction. Very slowly, I felt my way into the locker area and moved across to the wall that would take me to the door and, hopefully, the light switches.

My hands hit the door, and I breathed a sigh of relief. Running my hands over the wall on my left, I found a series of switches. I closed my eyes and turned them on. You have to do this gradually or you'll be temporarily blinded. And I needed every second if I was going to figure out how to get out of here.

Someone pounded on the door, and I jumped back.

"Merry?" Kelly's voice called out. "Please tell me you're in there!"

"Well, I'd love to tell you I was back home in bed with a good book," I responded. "But I can't, so you'll just have to settle for me being locked in here."

"Thank God!" Kelly sighed. "The lights went out here again, and when they came on, you were missing! We'd thought the worst!"

"Did you see who turned off the lights?"

I was pretty sure the answer was no.

"No, but Kevin was able to turn them back on."

Kevin again. I wondered if I could have him arrest himself? He'd probably do it.

Mitch's voice came forward. "Merry? Are you okay? I'd never forgive myself if something happened to you!"

"I think you can help," I replied. "The door opens to the inside of the locker room. I want you to try to kick it in. You'll have to hit it where the latch is."

"Right!" Mitch said. "Kevin! Jason! Brandon! Dylan! Let's break down this door!"

"I'm not doing that!" I heard Brandon say. "That door is too big!"

"Fine." Mitch tried again, "Jason, Kevin, and Dylan are with me!"

There was some murmuring going on on the other side of the door.

"Okay." Mitch sounded irritated. "Jason and Kevin are with me...what?" More murmuring. "Whatever! I'll do it myself! Back up, Merry!"

I moved off to the right, away from the door should it burst open. Something slammed hard against the door, and it started to give. There was a moan on the other side.

"Are you alright?" I asked Mitch. Hopefully, the answer would be yes, and he would continue to act as a battering ram to get me out.

"Um, yes," Mitch's voice sounded a little strangled. "Hold on."

I waited again. Why was he in pain? He should be fine just kicking it in. As long as he didn't use the shoulder he'd damaged earlier, it would work.

This time the door flew open and crashed against the wall. I ran out before it could swing shut. Mitch was standing off to the side, holding his shoulder. Kelly was feeling it. I'll bet she liked that.

"It's dislocated again. Hold on." Kelly popped it back into position.

He didn't even cry out. I'd have been proud of him had he been my boyfriend. Mitch rubbed his arm and thanked her.

"You hit it with your shoulder?" I wanted to tell him he was an idiot, but he had just rescued me. "Let me guess, you kicked it in the second time."

Mitch nodded. "I probably should've done that first."

I wondered. This guy has worked in construction for the past ten years. Wouldn't he know to kick it in in the first place?

Then again, maybe he had been so caught up in his macho crap that he wasn't thinking at all and decided it was more manly to use the same shoulder he had dislocated earlier.

Kelly turned her attention to me, appraising my physical situation. A quick glance at my wrists and she realized I'd been tied up. She didn't mention it, probably thinking I'd reveal what happened at some point.

She wasn't wrong. So far, only the killer and I knew I'd been tied up. Maybe that could work to my advantage.

Cindy came over as the others lost interest and faded away. "Merry, I have to tell you something." She looked around nervously. "Just before the lights went out, I saw Kevin near the locker room door."

I looked at the policeman, who was licking the empty chips bowl.

"I'm probably wrong," she said. "But I think he was on the stage just before I found Marla."

Kevin? Kevin who had the intellect of a lobotomized earthworm? Did earthworms have brains? They must. But how would you lobotomize one…oh, for crying out loud. I was losing my mind.

She waved me off. "I must be wrong. Kevin's a policeman. I swear, I'm looking at everyone as a suspect now. It's so hard to know who to trust, isn't it? I keep this up and I'll accuse myself as the killer."

As Cindy walked away, I had to admit she seemed terrified. And I had to admit that Kevin was the only one here with handcuffs. No. That was crazy. Kevin? A killer? I spotted him again, this time eating a napkin.

Wait, hadn't Kelly said Kevin was the one who turned on the lights? Was Kevin an evil mastermind who waited ten, I mean, eleven years to enact his revenge on his classmates? Had he been playing the role of an imbecile for more than a decade just so that he could kill Marla, Barry, and Amanda?

If he had, he was better than I thought. Like, by one thousand times better. It wasn't unheard of, I suppose. In the CIA, we had agents undercover for years waiting for the right intel. I, myself, was undercover with Carlos the Armadillo and Azlan, a Chechen strong man (who preferred to be called Wally).

But ten years?

Well, there was Gary. Gary had been a field agent who spent twelve years embedded with a Finnish health cult believed to be selling weapons illegally before he realized he'd gotten it wrong and was supposed to be embedded with a Swedish death cult who actually were fencing military-grade weapons. I guess anyone could mix that up…except for Swedes and Finns. Still, Gary hadn't freaked out. He was now stationed in the Arctic Circle until retirement, keeping an eye on polar bears and walruses. I'd heard he was very happy but did call Interpol from time to time, referring to the sketchy antics of a particular walrus named Big Pappy.

Kevin loped over to me. "Did you find any food in the locker room?"

"No," I said flatly. "Just a pair of handcuffs." I watched him carefully.

"What a coincidence." Kevin frowned. "I guess I left them in there. Maybe when this is done, I'll go look for my gun in that kids' park." He walked away.

He left them in there? Did Kevin just admit that he'd been in there when I was? Had he just admitted to being the killer?

CHAPTER NINETEEN

Kelly stared at me. "Kevin. Kevin Dooley. You think Kevin is the killer."

I ran my fingers through my hair. "I know. I'm totally losing it. I can't believe I suspect him."

"Suspect?" Kelly's right eyebrow went up. "Not suspected briefly while temporarily insane?"

We were sitting on the bleachers. Lucinda and Judy were putting the platters and bowls in a box, probably to keep Kevin from outright eating them. The others were talking quietly, casting furtive glances in our direction. Kevin was asleep on one of the mats.

"Cindy's right," I said. "It's impossible to know who to trust." I glanced at the girls, who were still asleep on their mat. "Except for you, of course. And Caterina, Lauren, and Ava."

"Thanks," Kelly said. "Not Betty?"

"I'm not going to rule it out." Okay, so I didn't really suspect Betty. What motive would she have for knocking off my classmates, other than an experiment for extra credit?

"One of *those* people"—Kelly pointed at the others—"is a killer. I'm sure they all have motives for wanting Marla dead. But Amanda and Barry? I don't get it."

"And you. And me," I added. "Except…they didn't kill either one of us."

"Do you think the killer is getting sloppy?" she asked. "Making mistakes?"

I shrugged. "Carried away and realizes now that there's a small suspect pool. But then, why risk the attacks on you and me?"

"Well, it's obviously not to frighten us into stopping the investigation, since that hasn't worked. Other than that, I have no idea." Kelly rubbed her eyes. "I was hoping you would figure it out and wrap it up soon."

"Aww. You have faith in me!" That felt good.

"Yeah." She nodded her head in the direction of our classmates. "But I don't think they do."

Ashley walked over, flanked by Dylan and Brandon.

"We want to talk to you," she said flatly. "We think you're the killer."

My jaw dropped. "What? Why?"

"You are running around trying very hard to find the killer. That's what a guilty person would do." She sniffed arrogantly.

"You're joking," I said. "You're saying that anyone not trying to find the killer is innocent."

"Of course," Ashley said.

Dylan and Brandon nodded behind her.

"You'd rather just sit here and allow yourselves to be picked off one by one?" I asked.

"No," Ashley reasoned. "Because now we know who the killer is. It's you. We just have to stay away from you."

"Why would I hit my best friend in the head?" I asked. Kelly agreed.

"To throw us off your trail, of course," Brandon sneered.

I toyed with punching him in his weasel face. But I thought that might make me look guilty. And I wasn't.

"Maybe *you* did it," Betty said quietly. I hadn't even noticed her waking up.

Ashley jumped backward as if bitten. "Why would I kill anyone? It doesn't make sense."

Betty leaned forward and whispered something that Ashley had to double over to hear. She stood up straight, her cheeks bright pink. Then she turned and walked back to the group, with Brandon and Dylan behind her.

"What did you say to her?" I asked.

Betty looked me in the eye. "It's better you don't know. Plausible deniability and all that."

Kelly interrupted before I could react. "This is getting out of hand. Now they suspect you. We need to end this before we all start killing each other and Kevin eats us."

"Ladies," Lauren called to get Kelly's and my attention. "May we draw your attention to the murder board?"

Ava and Caterina wheeled it over. Somehow, they had printed pictures of my conscious classmates. And they had all been detailed. Cindy's bleached teeth were blackened out. Lucinda had hairy warts, Judy had a full handlebar mustache, and Kevin had a unicorn horn. The rest were more of the same.

"How did you do this?" I asked as I admired Ashley's photo where she was sporting a sizeable Viking beard.

"Betty found a portable printer in the dressing room under the stage." Caterina beamed.

"And they all let you take their pictures?" I asked.

"Oh sure," Betty said. "People will let you do anything if they think you have the goods on them."

Uh-oh. "Betty, have you been telling people you have info on them?"

"Of course. How can I expect them to screw up?"

"That's dangerous! There's somebody here who has murdered three people!"

Lauren grinned. "Then we might flush them out!"

"I'll be the bait." Betty nodded. "And then when the killer tries to murder me, you catch him in the act."

She said it as if it was the most normal thing ever for me to offer up a eleven-year-old as murder bait.

I stood up and looked at the others across the gym. "If anyone here lays *one hand* on any of these girls," I shouted, "I will do terrible things to you with a fish fork! Understand?"

My classmates looked confused but nodded.

"A fork? How is that scary?" Ava demanded.

"It is if it's rusty," I said. "No more talking to the suspects!"

Kelly agreed. "Now you're on the killer's radar. That's not good."

"We'll do the buddy system." Caterina shrugged. "We'll never be away from our buddy."

"And then they can kill both of you," I insisted. "From here on out, you guys stick to me or Mrs. Albers like glue. Got it?"

Betty folded her arms over her chest. "Mrs. Albers got hit in the head, and you were tied up in the locker room. You seem less safe than the people asleep on the floor."

She had a point.

I shook my head. "Doesn't matter. Those are the rules. Alright?"

Cindy and Judy wandered over. "Merry, what's with the announcement?" Cindy asked.

"I want to make sure the killer doesn't target them," I explained.

"That would be horrible." Judy shuddered.

"Surely the killer wouldn't murder children." Cindy blanched.

"If they try," said Betty as she threw a couple of martial arts kicks and strikes into the air, "we'll take them down!"

That made the women laugh, something I don't think Betty was shooting for. Then they saw the murder board, complete with their photos.

"Nice mustache." Cindy poked Judy playfully.

"I'm jealous of your teeth," Judy laughed. "Or lack thereof."

The women began to laugh, and the girls were perplexed. Obviously, they hadn't counted on this sort of reaction.

"I like the board," Cindy said as she carefully wiped her eyes to avoid smudging her makeup.

Judy nodded. "Who's your main suspect?"

I wasn't quite sure what to say. Technically speaking, these two were suspects as well. But they had helped with pressing Brandon and Jason for info. I decided to go with that.

"Brandon and Jason are still wildcards." I glanced at Kelly, who shook her head. "The yearbooks weren't conclusive."

Judy picked up the book from our senior year and began browsing. Cindy looked over her shoulder.

"There." Judy pointed. "That's Jason." It was a candid of a boy and some other people sitting in the cafeteria. The kid was at a distance and in profile. Not a clear likeness.

"That's just a candid," Cindy said. "Find his class picture. It's Jason Hess, I think."

Judy flipped to the page and frowned. "It says *Photo Not Available*." She paged through all the class photos. "He's the only one like that."

"Hess," I muttered. His wallet had an Illinois driver's license that said Jason Hess. "He had a military ID that said Jason Grosz."

The women looked at me.

"How do you know that?" Judy asked.

"I saw it when he was getting money out for the cash bar," I explained breezily. "He took it out as if he was going to be carded then put it back." Could be true. "It was kind of weird. Who gets carded at a ten-year..."

"Eleventh..." Judy corrected.

"...class reunion?" Okay, so I got a little carried away with the story. I was a spy. Sue me.

Cindy and Judy found this an acceptable answer.

"Military IDs are pretty hard to get." Cindy chewed her lip. "Did it look like a forgery?"

I shook my head. "It looked legit. So which Jason is it?"

Judy searched through the rest of the yearbook but couldn't find another photo of Jason. She riffled through the junior and sophomore books with the same results.

"They all say *Photo Not Available*. All three years!" She frowned.

"Do you think Jason is an imposter?" Cindy looked at me earnestly. "Or a spree killer?"

Judy jumped on that. "A spree killer would make sense, motive wise. I still can't figure out a connection between the three victims."

Betty puffed up with pride but said nothing.

Neither could I. "We're missing something. What is it? What ties them together?"

Kelly, Cindy, and Judy looked thoughtful for a moment.

"Well," Kelly said slowly. "Marla, Barry, and Amanda were popular. They all were in the same clique."

I jumped on it. "That might be it! Marla was talking about secrets. What if there was something only the three of them knew?"

"Wouldn't she have put that in her speech?" Judy wondered.

Cindy shook her head. "Not if it implicated all three of them. There must've been some scandal that we can't remember."

"I can only think of pranks." I scratched my chin. "And they were kind of lame."

Kelly snapped her fingers. "Like the time all those chickens were let loose in the school!"

Cindy and Judy nodded.

"Oh," I said. "That was kind of me."

Cindy's eyebrows shot up. "It was?"

"Kind of?" Judy asked.

Kelly looked stormy. "And I didn't know about it?"

I threw up my arms. "It was embarrassing! I didn't tell anyone! There was a truck out back. I stopped to look inside and must have accidentally tripped the latch, because all these chickens came pouring out. I opened the door to run inside, and they all kind of swarmed me! And then I didn't want to shut the door on them because it might kill one, so I held it open."

Kelly's lips twitched as she suppressed a grin.

Betty was writing this down in her notebook. "The trick is to dye them school colors first."

We stared at her as the other girls nodded knowingly.

"You did that?" Kelly shook her head. "And you didn't tell your best friend?"

"I didn't want you to think I was an idiot."

"You are an idiot," Kelly said…affectionately, I think.

Cindy's eyes went wide. "Hey! Remember that car accident just outside of town? The one where that kid from Bladdersly was killed?"

"Oh yeah." Judy nodded. "Someone ran a stoplight and smashed into the other car. The kid who died lived long enough to say it was a white car with three kids inside!"

Kelly gasped. "Do you think Marla, Barry, and Amanda were those kids?"

"They never found out who did it," I said slowly.

"Marla had a white car," Judy said. "And her parents were rich enough to be able to get it fixed out of town so that no one would suspect."

"The killer found out somehow. Maybe Barry or Amanda confessed at some point." I thought this out. "Is it possible that Jason is an imposter from Bladdersly who infiltrated our reunion out of revenge?"

Judy shot a surreptitious look his way. "He could be a relative of the guy who died."

It seemed far-fetched and perfect all at the same time. But was it true?

Kelly shook her head. "I don't know, guys. They never proved who was driving the other car. It seems like a stretch to take all three victims here and put them in that car. And the kid who died could've been wrong."

"That idea is plausible." Cindy hesitated. "But that doesn't mean Jason did it."

"Why didn't he leave?" Betty asked. We all looked at her as if seeing her for the first time. "Why not kill them and go?"

"Because it would be suspicious," Lauren explained. "How could he explain that he somehow managed to get out of the locked gym if he wasn't the killer?"

She had a good point. If I were the killer, I'd stick around and act all innocent, to be freed when everyone else was.

"Yes, but did he think of that?" Judy pressed. "I like this theory. It answers everything."

"Why attack Kelly and Merry?" Cindy asked. "Why not kill them?"

Kelly offered up one of the ideas we'd considered earlier. "Maybe those incidents were warning us to stop investigating?"

I tried to recall the details from the accident. There were a lot of rumors flying around the school, but I didn't remember anyone in our class being blamed. Then again, I didn't pay a lot of attention back then, and I wasn't in the gossip grapevine.

"What do we do now?" Judy asked.

I leaned in. "You guys need to go back to the group and bring up the accident, very casually. See what Jason's reaction is."

Cindy nodded. "What are you going to do?"

"I'm going to have a chat with my ex-boyfriend."

CHAPTER TWENTY

It wasn't hard drawing Mitch away. It was hard getting the girls to stay at the table. I had to promise them they could handcuff the killer. Kevin would be disappointed, but I hoped it wouldn't be hard getting him to hand over the cuffs. And if he was the killer, he had no say in it anyway.

"At last." Mitch wiggled his eyebrows suggestively as I pulled him aside. "Some time alone with my best girl." He moved to put his arm around me.

"You touch me," I warned, "and I'll send you flying into that wall."

Mitch pulled back. "I've always liked that feisty side of you."

I rolled my eyes but didn't respond to that. "I need to know something. You were popular in high school. You hung out with the right crowd."

Mitch's eyes went wide. "Is that what this is about? My hidden shame back then that you weren't in the right social circle? I swear, it doesn't matter now. I don't care if you weren't in the same clique as me. I never did."

Talking to Mitch was becoming exhausting.

I held up my hand. "Forget all of that. I need to know something. About those days."

He gave me his most dazzling smile. "Anything for you!"

I reconsidered throwing him against the wall, preferably so that he'd hit it with his twice dislocated shoulder. Maybe later, when I had the intel I needed.

"Do you remember the car accident? The one that killed that kid from Bladdersly?"

Mitch scowled. "Why are you asking me about that?"

"Did you ever hear anything about it?"

"There were rumors, of course. But nothing concrete." He seemed edgy. Perhaps the whole in crowd swore a pact never to reveal the truth. Mitch shifted his weight from one foot back to the other. "I don't see any point in dredging up the past."

"I do," I said flatly. "It's possible this has to do with that."

He actually paled. "What do you mean?"

I laid it all out. "Were Marla, Barry, and Amanda in that car that night? Did they cause the accident?"

Mitch closed up. I knew that look. I'd seen it in Qatar when I was questioning a Russian operative. I'd seen it in Colombia when I was interrogating a drug lord. And I'd seen it over Ireland when a steward refused to give me a fourth glass of wine on a flight between Dublin and London.

I pressed him. "This is important, Mitch. I wouldn't ask if it wasn't. I don't want to shame anyone. In fact, if it is true, it doesn't matter because those three are dead."

Mitch became cold and aloof. "I don't want any part of this. It was a long time ago and isn't relevant. I'd be happy to make out with you. But I'm not going to say anything about the accident."

"I have absolutely no interest in making out with you, Mitch," I said firmly.

He threw his hands up in the air. "I don't know why you're doing this ridiculous investigation."

"Ridiculous? Three people are dead, my best friend was punched in the head. Someone tried to kill me and then tied me up in the locker room! I'd hardly call that ridiculous!"

"Whatever," he snapped. "This is something for the police. Not you." He turned and walked away.

"I agree!" I shouted after him. "Just wait until my husband gets here!"

The others turned to look at me, but Mitch continued walking away. In case Kelly, Cindy, and Judy were getting somewhere, I joined the girls at the table. A spy always knows when to walk away, whether you walked in on armed operatives in a secret room in the Canadian embassy or you've accidentally crashed Al-Qaeda's bowling night in Mogadishu.

"What did he say?" Betty asked me.

"Nothing," I grumped.

"Nothing like he refused to talk? Or nothing like you're blowing us off?" Ava asked.

"He didn't say anything. Refused to even talk about it."

Caterina said, "That's interesting. It makes him sound pretty guilty, doesn't it?"

Did it? Mitch could be covering for himself. Maybe he had been in there too, and he'd spotted the connection. That could be why he's sticking to me. It didn't implicate him in the murders necessarily. Or did it?

Maybe Mitch killed Marla, Barry, and Amanda because they were going to talk tonight? That seemed like a good motive to me. And by pretending a relationship we never had, he was trying to ingratiate himself into my circle to take suspicion away from him.

Whoa. This could break the case wide open. Suddenly, I felt very, very tired. I wished Mitch were right, that my gorgeous detective husband could be here handling this instead of me. I was spending more time in one night with some of these people than I had in all four years of high school.

And I didn't want to anymore. Slumping in my chair, I considered my options—my favorite being just sitting here until the night janitor unlocked the gym. Suspecting and fighting my classmates was wearing me out. Why not just give up?

"I'm right," Betty said as she sharpened one end of a flagpole into a spike. "About Mitch."

"You just might be." Where had she gotten that knife? "What are you doing, exactly?"

Betty didn't stop. "I'm going to make a fort for us to stay in until the cavalry comes. This is for the palisades."

"Betty's been watching Westerns," Ava said.

"But there's only one pole," Lauren admitted. "So we're going to bust up some chairs and tables to make more."

"Ah," I sighed. "Proceed."

"Merry?" Kelly asked as she walked over. "Why is Betty making a weapon?"

Uh-oh. Was I being an irresponsible adult? I took the knife the kid had set aside.

"Because why wouldn't you make weapons?" Betty asked without looking up. She was sanding it now. And doing a good job of it too.

"Okay, here." I started to hand the knife back, but Kelly intercepted. "Hey," I protested, "she might need that."

Kelly sat down, recognizing my mood. "Okay. If you don't want to hear what we've found out, that's fine."

I looked at her.

"Amanda was in the car. Ashley confirmed it. But she wasn't driving. Want to guess who was?"

It popped into my mind. "Mitch."

Kelly's face fell a little. "How did you know?"

"It was a hunch."

She sat down next to me. "So why the long face?"

"I don't want to do this anymore. I don't want to know these things about people I haven't been interested in seeing over the past eleven years. This is getting twisted. And I don't care about those people. I only care about you and the kids."

"What about Marla? Barry? Amanda?" Kelly asked. "What about justice?"

"This just feels so wrong. Digging into everyone's sordid past. Looking for long-dead secrets."

"Just like the stuff you did as a spy," Kelly replied.

That drew me up short.

"Betty keeps a notebook full of secrets on the kids at school," Lauren offered.

Ava nodded. "She's got some stuff in there you wouldn't believe."

Kelly spoke up. "That's a bad idea." She turned back to me. "Why not just give everyone the benefit of the doubt? You'll just turn into a bitter, resentful woman like Marla. She lived to come here and blab on everyone."

I pulled the speech out and waved it. "And look how she ended up. Marla was killed for keeping secrets and maybe for this piece of paper. I…"

A few words at the bottom of the page caught my eye. I opened it and read. My spydy sense was tingling. Actually, it was vibrating. I got up and looked at the trash can that Kelly and the others had used to clean up. I walked over to it and studied the contents. Then I looked at my cell.

"Did you take all these photos on my phone?" I asked as I pulled up individual pictures.

"Yup," Caterina said as something caught her attention. "Hey! People are waking up!"

"Can we interview them?" Lauren asked eagerly. "We need to know stuff for our report."

My mind was elsewhere, so I waved them away. I heard Betty ask one of my classmates, "How are you feeling? Angry? Confused? Does your butt hurt from lying on the hard floor so long?"

Ava's voice added, "We have a little waiver you'll need to sign. You don't need to read it first."

Of course they had some sort of nondisclosure agreement. Normally, I'd check that out, but my heart was beating faster, and my adrenaline was starting to spike as I swiped through all the photos. When I found the right one, I enlarged it. And smiled. After scanning through the pictures the girls said they'd taken earlier in the night, I found the answer to a question that had been bugging me. Why hadn't I checked this sooner! Oh well. My disappointment was overshadowed by the fact that I'd cracked the case. That was good enough for me.

I stood up and waved Kevin over. I didn't want to wait for the night janitor one minute more.

Kevin stepped up, and I said, "It's time to get out of here, don't you think?"

"Well, yeah." He looked half asleep. "There's no food."

I sympathized as my stomach rumbled again. "See if you can find me something I can use as a sort of battering ram."

Kevin loped away.

"You know who did it." Kelly smiled.

"I know who did it." I smiled back. "We need to get out of this gym and call the police. Once they get here, I'll tell you what I know."

I got up and walked to the main set of doors with Kelly and the girls behind me. Everyone else got quiet, and I heard footfalls heading my way.

Kevin appeared, holding a large fire axe. "I couldn't find a battering ram. All I could find is this. Sorry."

I stared at the axe before swinging it over my shoulder. I didn't even yell at him for not finding it sooner as I took a swing at the door.

CHAPTER TWENTY-ONE

The last blow from the axe destroyed the door bar. I kicked the door open and walked into the lobby with everybody else following behind me. We must have looked a sight—a disheveled group of adults busting through the doors with me in the lead and a large fire axe over my shoulder.

Standing there was my husband. Rex's jaw dropped open. Which was surprisingly satisfying.

"What are you doing here?" I asked my husband then turned to the group. "Nobody leaves! Not until I tell you all what really happened."

I wanted to jump into his arms, but we had an agreement not to do stuff like that when he was working. I honestly didn't think he'd mind, considering the situation, but I wanted my classmates to take me seriously, so I fought off the urge.

Everyone just looked at me dully, and then they went back inside the gym. I guess, knowing that the doors were open and the police were here, they thought what's a few more minutes? I was pretty sure that everyone was curious about what had really happened tonight…even the killer would want to know if I'd figured it out.

My husband watched my classmates file back inside. "It's the middle of the night. Robert and I couldn't get through to you or Kelly. Our calls went straight to voicemail. I called the station and had a cruiser drive by, and they said the lot was still full." He cocked his head to the side. "But I had the feeling something was wrong. I can't really explain it."

I handed him the fire axe. "But you came from Reno! How did you get a commercial flight so quickly?"

Rex shook his head. "I didn't. The lieutenant governor was in town and offered to give me a ride back on his private plane." He looked me up and down again. "You look hot, in a kind of third world zombie apocalypse way."

I smiled. "That's nothing. Wait till you get a load of the three dead bodies inside!"

His eyebrows went up. "Three? You're upping your game. But did you have to lock them all in the gym so well that you needed an axe to get out?"

"Yeah, that wasn't me. Come on." I turned and went back into the gym. I wanted to say I love you, but I think Rex knew that without me saying it in front of everyone.

"I'll call forensics," he said. "Then I'll be right there."

All fifty of my classmates sat around the tables, and I stood in the middle of the gym. Those who'd been on the floor still looked a little dazed. Cindy and Judy had gently broken the news to everyone about Marla, Barry, and Amanda while I was in the lobby with Rex. They were too foggy to really take it all in, except for Eddy, who was quietly crying over the loss of his best friend.

When Rex joined me, I quietly told my husband about the doping but did not mention the girls. I'd leave that to his discretion when I told him all the details later. While Kelly and the girls stood off to the side, Rex gave Officer Kevin Dooley instructions, and he held his handcuffs at the ready, happy to not be in charge. We'd been joined by Thad Murray, Rex's newest officer, newly returned from the police academy. It was nice to have this much firepower at my back, even though, in a pinch, Betty could've handled it with her flag spike.

"Whenever you're ready." Rex gestured toward the floor, indicating I had it.

"This," I said as I turned to the group and waved at everything around me, "was a total dumpster fire. Seriously, I'm never going to another reunion again."

There was a murmur of agreement. My classmates who'd missed the whole thing seemed to be glad that they had. They wouldn't be once Betty posted their LSD antics on social media. I'd try to stop her, but that kid would probably find ways around it. It was something I'd have to worry about later.

I continued, "Thanks for sticking around. I'll get straight to it. From the start, I had this all wrong, which is really annoying by the way."

"Tell me about it," Betty and Lauren said in unison.

I ignored them. "After proving that this wasn't just an accident, I'd thought that this was just a simple revenge murder. Well, it was, and it wasn't. The sad fact of the matter is Marla Zimmer was a terrible person."

My classmates nodded. In fact, there wasn't one single person who disagreed. Which was kind of sad.

I went on. "Marla was determined to make all of us squirm. And why? She'd had everything. From class president to prom queen—if there was some prize to be won, she won it. And yet, it didn't make her happy. She had decided to torment almost all of us at our own reunion, which tells us she was a miserable person."

Again, my classmates nodded.

"And so she made this big presentation where she told us she had some secrets to reveal about us, in a speech that would take place later. She twisted the knife, and it worked. Somebody, who'd probably been wanting to do this for a long time, found their chance to take Marla out once and for all."

Kelly gave me that look that said *hurry it up, please*. And since she had a goose egg on the back of her head, I decided to comply. Besides, I was dirty and tired. I wanted a hot bubble bath and a bottle of wine followed by a week in bed, curled up with the handsome detective standing nearby.

"But she didn't give the speech," Eddy said.

"We found it," Mitch said. "Merry read it to us—just the parts about the ones who were still coherent. Believe me, you should be glad you were passed out."

Veronica glared. "It was just a bunch of stupid lies. And why is *she* getting to tell us? I still think Merry did it!"

The first thing I was going to do Monday morning was call whatever the governing board for real estate agent was and tell them what Marla had said. Even if it wasn't true, Veronica would be on the hot seat until she proved otherwise.

"Here's what happened," I said. "Those of you who lived it will just have to bear with me a moment." I cleared my throat. "It all started with the speech Marla gave…"

"Don't forget the ninja janitor who locked us all in," Ava offered.

I gave her a nod and went through everything, starting with Marla's speech, the ninja janitor, Marla's murder, and a very skeletal description of the doping of our classmates that didn't implicate the girls in any way. I told them about finding Barry and Amanda's death. I might have made people sound a little more heroic than they were, but some of them deserved it after what they'd been through. I did leave out the part about Mitch hitting on me all night. It was yet one more thing I'd explain to my husband later.

Rex seemed more amused than alarmed about the cutting of the rope. His face showed serious concern, however, about Kelly's and my own assault in the locker room. I didn't go through Marla's accusations because we'd promised not to say anything. In fact, if Rex didn't need it, I might burn the whole thing after letting Kelly read it, just for fun.

"This is all crap!" Veronica slammed her hand on the table.

I took a moment to check out the others. Jason and Brandon still sat together. When people had come to, no one had gone over and talked to either man. I didn't reveal the thing about Brandon's and Jason's wallets. I'd deal with that later.

"And then Kevin found a fire axe," I explained. "And I chopped down the door."

At that moment, the night janitor walked into the gym. He looked at the medical examiner checking out Barry's corpse and Amanda covered with a kimono against the wall. He looked at the door that had been smashed and a room full of disheveled people. It looked more like a street fight than a reunion. Then he noticed the police.

"Nope," he said, before dropping his mop, turning, and walking out of the room.

"We had lots of theories." I brought everyone's attention back to the task at hand. "From a car accident ten..."

"Eleven," Cindy corrected with a wink.

"Eleven years ago." I watched as Mitch squirmed in his seat. "To old grievances, to secrets that had to remain hidden, to even Officer Kevin Dooley here." I gestured to the man, who was eating a bag of chips with a look of euphoria on his face.

Cindy gave me a small smile. "I gave him money for the vending machine."

"You suspected Officer Dooley?" Thad Murray seemed shocked.

Rex shook his head at him, and he said nothing more. Thad hadn't really had much time to get to know the most, or least (depending on how you looked at it), "interesting" member of the force. That would come soon enough, and I hoped he'd stick around after that.

Rex asked me to go on, and I did. "We've been chasing this killer all night. And boy, did I get it wrong in the beginning."

"Who was it?" Kevin asked before shoving a fistful of chips into his mouth.

I looked over at Kelly, who was pulling up a chair. She looked a little dizzy. Oh, crap. She'd been concussed. This was wearing her out. Rex had called for an ambulance, but it hadn't arrived yet. I needed to wrap this up. I turned to the killer.

"Cindy, you killed Marla. You'd been planning it for years because of the constant torture she'd put you through in school. It wasn't a crime of opportunity like we'd thought with Barry and Amanda."

Cindy's jaw fell open. "You're joking! I didn't do it!"

"She's blaming you for *her* guilt!" Veronica said.

I pointed at her. "Veronica, shut up, or Lucinda is going to do some digging into your past." I glanced at Lucinda, who touched her hair and nodded with an eager grin.

Veronica sat back, arms folded across her chest, glaring at me.

"Why are you accusing Cindy?" Dylan looked around. "You've been best buds all night."

I nodded. "And that's what threw me off. It's quite simple really. Cindy was the only one onstage when she discovered Marla." I looked directly at her. "I'm guessing you lured her up there with something like adjusting the stage lights to make her look better and needing her help. Was that it?"

Cindy continued to look confused and horrified all at once.

"What I didn't know was that the girls had gotten hold of my phone and were taking pictures early in the night. And besides one hundred and seven selfies of Betty making rude gestures…" I looked at the kid. "We'll talk about that later, by the way."

Betty shrugged.

I went on. "She had a picture of you and Marla heading backstage. And a few minutes later, you came back out onstage. See, the thing is, the girls were holding the picture button down and taking a lot of photos. Two seconds after you emerged, you went backstage again. The next photo is me jumping up on stage because I heard you scream."

"That's all you've got on her?" Judy seemed doubtful. "It doesn't really seem like much in the way of proof."

I nodded. "I'm sure when the forensics team starts fingerprinting everything from the ladder to the rails on the catwalk and the beam holding the counterweight, they'll find her prints."

Brandon raised his hand. "Surely she'd wear gloves, right?"

I shook my head. "I never found any. So I realized she probably wouldn't if she thought it would be considered an accident. If it was an accident, no one might ever check. By the time they did, she'd be halfway to Kansas City, or wherever she's really from."

Lucinda cocked her head to the side. "Okay, so if that's true, what made Cindy decide to kill Barry and Amanda? Were they premeditated too?"

"How could I have killed Barry when I was backstage with you and the girls the whole time?" Cindy asked innocently.

I shook my head. "Cindy didn't kill Barry and Amanda." I waited for that to sink in.

"But you said…" Jason started, but I cut him off.

"I said that Cindy killed Marla. I didn't say she'd murdered everyone."

A strange silence descended over the room as my classmates realized that they'd been hanging out with more than one killer. To me, the realization had been a relief because I hadn't been able to put all the murders together to find a motive. Two of the killings in any combination might make sense, but with the exception of the car accident theory, I couldn't connect the third death.

I was sad to out Cindy. She'd seemed like the only sane person there. Well, until I knew she'd killed Marla, that is.

Ashley looked around and asked, "Then who killed Barry and Amanda?"

I pointed to someone at the next table. "Eddy killed Barry."

The large man blanched. "But I was unconscious!"

"That's what you'd like us to think." I nodded. "And I almost didn't see it."

Mitch looked sideways at his friend. "Eddy was faking being passed out the whole time?"

I nodded. "Yup. I inadvertently saw Eddy's name on the speech and read what Marla had written. Lucinda had been talking about it earlier, and I didn't see it. But the real tip-off came from the crime scene photos the girls had taken."

"You're welcome," Betty said.

Caterina nodded. "We totally solved this."

I gave them the thumbs-up and continued. "Those who'd been drugged, dropped their cups on the floor when they started hallucinating. Everyone who drank the punch had a cup next to them on the floor. But one was missing. I confirmed it when I counted the cups in the garbage. And in the pictures the girls took, there wasn't a cup near him. Eddy hadn't had the punch."

"But we saw him," Judy said. "He was just as crazy as the others."

"I think when people started freaking out, Eddy saw an opportunity and went along with it, thinking this was his moment. He'd brought a weapon with him but wasn't sure how or when to use it on Barry. Then, when he saw the others fall to the floor, he did too. When he noticed that the rest of us were backstage, he killed Barry, threw the garrote at the stage, then assumed the position on the floor."

I pulled out the speech with the garrote in it and handed it over to Rex, who used a handkerchief to take it from me. "You used leather grips. And since you're not wearing any gloves, I'll bet your fingerprints are all over them."

Lauren stepped up. "He threw it onto the stage to frame one of you guys!"

Eddy sighed and rubbed his neck. He wasn't cut out for a life of crime. "It was painful too," he admitted. "I had to lie there until at least one other classmate came to. And I still got busted."

Judy asked, "Why did he do it? Barry was his best friend. Right?"

It was messed up. I'd never kill Kelly—not for any reason. "I remembered Lucinda talking about Heather, Barry's wife, who we'd all gone to school with. What I read in Marla's speech was that Barry stole Eddy's girlfriend our sophomore year, and it broke his heart. And then Barry married her after high school. I'm guessing when Heather divorced Barry, Eddy really believed she'd come back to him. But she didn't."

Eddy exploded. "She did *everything* for him, and he screwed around on her. I kept waiting for Heather to see sense and come back to me. Instead, she ran off to India, joined a commune, and has some other boyfriend who's a swami! I waited for *years* for Heather to realize I was the only love she'd ever had. But no, she decided to throw away all those years. And you know what Barry did when I told him that? He laughed. He called me a sore loser. He said he was waiting for me to get another girlfriend so that he could steal her from me and marry her too. I hated him for that. When I had the chance to kill him, I took it." He took several deep breaths and calmed down. "I've never hurt anyone before. But if I had the chance to do it all again, I'd still kill that bastard."

Kelly was starting to slump forward, and Rex spotted it. The EMTs made an appearance, and he waved them over. I needed to wrap this up. I looked over and saw Kevin positioned behind Cindy, eating a bag of Cheetos. He was going to get that orange dust all over her when he cuffed her. I was looking forward to seeing that.

Thad had moved over to stand next to Eddy so that he could cuff him later. I felt a little sad about him too. How awful to have what you think is your one chance at love stolen by your jerk of a best friend?

Judy's voice brought me back to the present. "What about Amanda? Did Eddy kill Amanda? I think we'd have noticed an unconscious guy of his size doing that."

I sighed. Most of the time I was happy for the killer to get their just desserts. This night was different.

"Her twin, Ashley, killed Amanda. Before they came to the reunion, Ashley spiked Amanda's sinus inhaler with some sort of poison. Actually, I think there were two spiked inhalers. I believe she'd intended to blame Marla by planting one of the inhalers in her purse. When Marla was murdered, Ashley figured she'd just blame the killer."

Ashley burst out in tears. Dylan didn't know if he should comfort her or move away. After a split second, he put his arm around her. I didn't know how he was going to manage a convicted murderer girlfriend in prison while running for office, but this was Iowa, and stranger things have happened.

"What happened to Amanda's other inhaler?" Brandon asked.

Now I was glad I hadn't searched her purse. "Ashley was next to the body while Kelly was giving her CPR. She most likely pocketed it."

Happy for something to do, Kevin brightened, walked away from Cindy, searched Ashley, and produced the inhaler. He seemed disappointed, like he'd expected to find something to eat. Rex called out, but it was too late. The inhaler was covered in Cheeto dust. It didn't help that, when he noticed, he started licking the inhaler.

Rex walked over and took it from him as Thad watched in horror.

Eddy was genuinely surprised. "Why did she do it?"

Ashley jumped to her feet, hands curled into fists. "Because *she* was the *pretty* one! She got all the attention because she was so gorgeous!"

Jason spoke up. "Um, hate to break it to you, but you're identical twins."

Ashley's face was red with fury. "I know, right? I never liked my sister! When we made cheerleader, she made captain! When we were on the homecoming and prom courts, she was one position ahead of me! She even had a better GPA! I hated her!"

"But you told me you didn't like doing those things," Lucinda said. "You said you never wanted to be a cheerleader or homecoming queen."

Ashley began to tremble with rage. "I didn't! But if I was going to, I should've gotten the leading role at least once! Amanda was never going to give up her power! She even made store manager last week at the mall! I'd have to work for her! That's when I decided to end this."

"Wow." Brandon whistled. "Three killers and three different motives. And all of them were premeditated too. Good job, Merry."

Was that a compliment? Now I really felt bad I didn't remember him.

There was a moment of silence, and then we all turned to Cindy, the one person who hadn't confessed.

Lucinda didn't take her eyes off of the beautiful blonde. "Then *she* locked us in here?"

"I think so. I'm willing to bet that she has the keys on her." I walked over to her and frisked her. Even turned her purse inside out. There was only a set of car keys that were easily identifiable.

"I didn't kill Marla, and I didn't orchestrate all this," Cindy insisted. "Did you drink the punch, Merry?"

"Aw," Lucinda said. "I kind of liked that you killed Marla. I wish I had."

Our classmates nodded.

"Then it wasn't about the secrets she was about to spill?" Kelly pushed away the EMT, holding up a finger to indicate she needed a second.

I shook my head. I had a backup theory. "No. They just hated Marla."

"They?" Jason and Brandon asked in unison.

I walked over to Judy. She tried to fight me off, but I put her in a headlock and nodded to Kevin. He took his sweet time to come over, but in her purse, he found a set of keys labelled *Gym, Lobby, Locker Room*. Once again, they were coated in Cheeto dust. Rex didn't even sigh as he confiscated those too. Thad Murray just shook his head. I'd have to let him know not to leave food around the office.

Lucinda frowned. "But she emptied her purse in front of us, and those keys weren't in there."

I shrugged. "She hid them somewhere. She's got pockets all over her suit, and we didn't pat her down because she voluntarily offered things up." My theory was a bit weak here, but hey, I found the keys on her! That was enough.

"Judy was in on it?" Kelly asked.

"She's the one who cut the rope." I released the woman.

Cindy shook her head. I really didn't like how calm she was. "That's ridiculous. What's her motive?"

"She hated Marla too. My guess is that Cindy approached Judy and told her what she wanted to do at the reunion. Judy agreed to help. Although I didn't suspect her until I found the remote that turned off the gym lights in the trash can. She was the only one we know handled the can. It would've been easy for her to throw it away. And I'll bet there are prints on that too."

Judy's eyes narrowed. "We would've gotten away with it if Eddy and Ashley hadn't screwed up!"

Cindy warned her, "Judy, don't say anything."

Judy broke free and glared at her partner. "No. If we're going to be dragged off to jail, I want to explain here and now." She turned to me. "Marla was awful. But she did something to me back in high school that I could never forgive. She got me expelled for smoking pot. And the funny thing is, it was her weed! She was the one who'd been smoking it, and she framed me!"

"You were the ninja janitor. The only thing I don't know," I continued, "was why you locked us in."

"That was my idea, and Cindy didn't think it would work." Judy ran her hands over her suit to smooth it. "It seemed like a good idea to give you all a much bigger problem to deal with instead of Marla's death. By the time we got out, everyone would've scattered to the four winds, making an investigation more difficult." She pointed at Cindy. "She has a beach house in Nicaragua. She got it from the husband she killed."

"That was true?" Ashley asked. "Cindy married a rich guy and killed him? Like Marla's speech said?"

Judy didn't say another word as Cindy fumed in silence. She never should've implicated Kevin. That was a mistake. It wasn't possible for Kevin to be an evil mastermind with a devious plan.

"I believe that it was Cindy who tackled me in the locker room and, using handcuffs she'd lifted from Kevin, handcuffed me to the bench and locked the door. There should be a set of night vision goggles in the locker room. My guess is they're hidden in one of the lockers."

Kevin stopped eating and looked down at his belt. When he saw that the cuffs were there, he shrugged and went back to eating. Rex's eyebrows went up, and I decided I'd give Kevin a chance to find his gun without telling Rex about it. Unless someone got shot with it. Then he was on his own.

"Is that why you killed Marla, Cindy?" Kelly asked. "To keep her from revealing a secret about you?"

Cindy said nothing. We looked at Judy, who just shrugged.

"Who hit Kelly on the head?" Lucinda asked. "Did someone try to kill her too?"

This was an idea, but it wouldn't change the fact that Cindy had murdered Marla. "I think Judy hit the remote, turning off the lights, and Cindy smacked Kelly in the head to distract me from investigating."

Cindy narrowed her eyes at me. Judy nodded, but said nothing.

Eddy spoke up. "I'm not sucking up or anything, but I think Mitch should get in trouble too."

"Me?" Mitch looked stunned. "Why?"

Eddy pointed at him. "Because I was sick and tired of hearing you feed Merry all that crap about being in love with her. It was bad enough I was trapped on the floor for hours, but having to listen to that too? You never mentioned her in high school. You're such a phony."

I glanced at Rex, whose eyebrows went up.

"What was that all about anyway?" I asked.

Mitch looked sheepish. "You didn't do *anything* in high school, and then you go off to live this exciting life. My life is boring as hell. Things were better in high school. I thought that if I pressed it, you'd believe it's true or, at least, would want to. But you didn't buy it for a second."

For some reason, I wasn't mad. Maybe I was just relieved to find out the truth, or maybe I was relieved to find out he didn't have a thing for me.

"Like I said," I reiterated. "I'm done with class reunions. So that's it. That's all I've got. The police will need to take your statements, so stick around."

I sat down in a chair as if I hadn't sat in days. The weight of the evening's activities slid away and took everything out of me.

"No more reunions, eh?" Kelly asked as she sat down next to me.

"Nope. And I don't advise it for you either."

"I'm okay," Kelly said. "But the EMTs suggested I stay with someone tonight, just in case." She gave me a questioning look.

Four little girls pooled around her. "That's why we're having a slumber party at your house, Mrs. Albers," Betty said. "We know first aid, and we're wide awake!"

"Great," Kelly groaned. "I'll be up all night with these four. Join me?"

I looked at Rex, who nodded.

"Sure. After three murders and an attempt on my co-leader, what more could go wrong?" I thought sadly about my shower and bed. But Kelly would have wine and food so that was a good trade-off. "I just need to pick up some pajamas at home." I looked at Mitch and said a little louder, "And make out with my husband." I turned back to Kelly. "And I'll be right over."

Rex took me aside. "You've had quite a night. Two attempts to kill you, three bodies, murderous classmates, and the old school quarterback hitting on you." He reached down and squeezed my hand.

I squeezed back. "Hard to believe that a class reunion could be so interesting, right?"

My husband laughed, and it washed over me like a tonic. "I forgot that Kevin graduated with you. How did it go having Officer Dooley here?"

I looked at Kevin, who was walking a handcuffed Cindy out, guzzling a cup of punch he'd pulled out of the trash can.

"He did okay. It was good to have him here."

Rex seemed more surprised by that than he had been by anything else tonight. "Really?"

I suppressed the memory of Kevin twerking when this all began. In spite of that, I said, "Yes, really."

And then I collapsed into my husband's arms.

CHAPTER TWENTY-TWO

Two days later, I was feeling like my old self again. Cindy had finally confessed to Marla's murder. It was hard to believe that the reunion took out seven people, one way or another.

Lucinda broke the story of the whole evening on the news and announced she was writing a true crime book on the subject. She's titling it *Memories Are Murder*. I thought it had a nice ring to it.

Veronica admitted to the national association of real estate agents that she might have forgotten to finish her education to receive her license. They gave her one month and said they wouldn't punish her if she pulled it off. I hope she gets it. I also hope I never have to run into her again. But it's a small town, so the odds aren't great.

As for my other classmates? There were no lingering LSD side effects, and to my surprise, none of them had pressed for an investigation. I suspected that Betty sent them her video footage and that shut them up, but I have no evidence of that.

"What about the girls drugging the punch with LSD?" I asked my husband as we lounged on the couch with our cats, Philby and Martini, and our Scottish deerhound, Leonard. Philby was sitting on my stomach, staring unblinkingly into my eyes as, every two seconds, she smacked me in the face. It was good to be home.

Rex sighed. "Through my investigation, I've deduced that Marla actually spiked the punch in order to further humiliate her classmates."

I grabbed hold of Philby's paw in mid-punch and set the rotund feline führer on the floor. "Oooh! I like that ending."

Rex brushed a stray curl from my eyes. "Well, I can't let my junior detectives get in trouble for that."

I sat up straighter—something easier to do when you don't have a twenty-pound cat on you. "You really have a junior detective program? And you are including my troop?"

He laughed and shook his head. "No way. Betty walks such a fine line between good and potential criminal that it would be dangerous to allow her near anyplace that housed weapons or sensitive files."

I leaned back into the couch. "I have to have a chat with Hilly about providing my troop with hallucinogens and the recipe for drugging a bunch of old people."

Rex agreed. "Yes, you do. I'd like to say I'm surprised that she did that, but I know better."

"It was pretty smart that they added melatonin," I grudged. "I don't know what I'd have done if I'd had forty more people to deal with. And it did narrow the suspect pool."

"I don't think you should mention that to the girls," he said. "It might only encourage them. Still, you did a good job with what you had. We did find Cindy's prints on the catwalk, Judy's prints on the remote, and Eddy's prints on the garrote. The inhaler was too damaged by Cheeto dust, but Ashley confessed to everything at the station, so we shouldn't need that for it to stick."

My husband looked like he was going to say something.

"You want the speech."

"I want the speech." He nodded. "I won't make the details public. But since the anchorwoman classmate of yours knows what's on there, she will probably include it in the book she's writing."

I handed it over. I'd been carrying it in my jeans pocket for two days, trying to decide what to do. I couldn't control Lucinda breaking her word. The book would be a lot juicier for it because everyone had some secret in there.

But if the anchorwoman came around asking for it, I wanted to be able to tell her it was in police custody. It wouldn't be impossible for her to get access to it, but the fact that it was evidence in four court cases would put her off for at least a while.

Rex opened the speech and began scanning it.

"You know," I interrupted. "I was so convinced Jason had crashed the reunion. I didn't get a chance to study the yearbooks. I don't suppose you looked into his alter ego, Jason Grosz?"

My husband gave me a strange look. "I did. It's classified. Jason is CIA. The only thing they'd tell me was he was there watching someone."

"Why didn't you tell me?" I gaped.

"I didn't want you to start reading anything into it," Rex said.

Too late. "It must be me! The CIA has someone watching me? Why?"

"It may not be you at all," Rex said. "I'm sure your friend Ahmed might be able to find out for you. I'm washing my hands of it. I have three murder investigations to pursue." He tapped the speech. "By the way, just from the first few lines, I can see that you have some mildly terrifying classmates."

I felt a twinge of guilt. "I do feel guilty about one thing," I admitted. "Brandon was just a blank in my mind. And yet his mannerisms were a bit familiar. I feel bad that nobody remembered him. How awful to go to your reunion and have people act like they never knew you existed."

Rex's eyebrows flew up. "Oh, right! I forgot! Brandon asked me to hand this to you." My husband walked out of the room. He returned with an envelope that he handed to me.

The envelope was labelled *For Merry's Eyes Only*. My spydy senses were tingling. I tore it open and began to read. The handwriting was very familiar, but not in the way I thought.

Merry, I'm so sorry I had to fool you like that. But I had to be certain that you were still, you know, you. And from the madness the other night, I realized you hadn't changed a bit. By the way, your classmates suck. No offence. Your troop, I'm sure, is still adorable. Tell them hi for me.

Why am I here? I need your help. I am very happy that disguising myself as Brandon worked. I've been working on new mask technology, and this one really paid off. I felt a little guilty about deceiving you, but you had your hands full, so it was better not to dump this on you too.

Why did I crash your reunion disguised as a dude? Because I'm in trouble. Big trouble. Please call this number first thing tomorrow morning. You are the only one I can turn to. And tell no one I've made contact.
    ~ Your old friend,
Maria

I re-read the letter over and over. Maria was a good friend from my CIA days and even helped me with a couple of cases afterward. Then she betrayed the agency for what she believed were the right reasons and vanished from the face of the Earth. I hadn't seen or spoken to her in a while.

And now here she was, out of the blue, asking for help.

I had to wonder, was Jason there to watch me or her? I picked up the phone and plugged her information into it, using a pseudonym, and set an alarm for 6 a.m. I had an important call to make, and nothing was going to make me miss it.

"Merry?" Rex looked up from the speech. "What's this about you letting a flock of chickens loose in the school? Did you know it caused $1500 in damage? That's what it says, anyway."

I stuffed the letter into the sofa cushions and leaned forward and kissed him. "How about we make a deal and you lose that part of the speech?"

He didn't answer as he pulled me against him. But I was pretty sure that was a yes.

ABOUT THE AUTHOR

Leslie Langtry is the *USA Today* bestselling author of the *Greatest Hits Mysteries* series, the *Merry Wrath Mysteries,* the *Aloha Lagoon Mysteries,* and several books she hasn't finished yet, because she's very lazy.

Leslie loves puppies and cake (but she will not share her cake with puppies) and thinks praying mantids make everything better. She lives with her family and assorted animals in the Midwest, where she is currently working on her next book and trying to learn to play the ukulele.

To learn more about Leslie, visit her online at:
http://www.leslielangtry.com

Enjoyed this book? Check out these other reads available now from Leslie Langtry:

www.GemmaHallidayPublishing.com

Made in United States
North Haven, CT
21 September 2022